YOUNG A
BY D. L. F

The Bird with the Broken Wing
Resident Spy
One Little Spell

~ Dedication ~

To Helen:
Too well-loved to ever be forgotten.

To Ian:
A wonderful husband who shares my dreams.

The Bird with the Broken Wing

D. L. Richardson

First electronic publication: September 2011, Etopia Press
First print publication: October 2012, Etopia Press

Second electronic publication: September 2014
Second print publication: October 2014

Prologue

She was a chronic worrier—

"I have a bad feeling about this, Ben."

—and a touch melodramatic.

"This is suicide. It's also stupid, morally wrong, and pointless. And did I mention suicide?"

Ben wasn't listening. He was reaching a hand inside the open neck of his shirt. She'd spent enough time with him to know he was touching the cross on the necklace that had once belonged to his dad.

"Detached, that's how you make me feel, Ben. Like I'm watching your life through a window."

Striking up an old conversation about how she felt isolated was hardly creative, yet the feeling of not belonging with him was stronger than ever. She gave a heavy, audible sigh but Ben wasn't taking the bait.

"A bubble. I live in a bubble."

"Relax." Ben closed his eyes as he sucked up a deep, dusty red breath like he was meditating on Mars. "Everything will be all right."

As well as a chronic worrier and a touch melodramatic, she was also an eternal optimist. So she looked around in case she was missing something, but all she saw was proof to the contrary. She, Ben, and a few hundred others were in a convoy, crossing a desert that appeared to be empty, yet the drivers had dodged gun and mortar fire since they'd passed over the border an hour ago.

What this land must have looked like when it had been fertile with lush, green trees and wide, blue rivers was hard to imagine, but she tried. Her eyes had closed for a second when a burst of gunfire to her right jolted them wide open again.

She scowled at him and said, "We signed up for non-combat jobs, remember?"

She wondered if punching him in the head would do any good. Probably not. If her bubble-hands were too weak to smash through the invisible wall surrounding her, they'd be like wet rags against his thick skull. Plus he was wearing a metal helmet and she was likely to break more than a nail.

"We're meant to be back home making trucks. That's what we were promised we'd be doing. Jeez, Ben. Think about your mom."

Perhaps he was. Perhaps many of the soldiers on the truck were thinking about loved ones they'd left behind. Many of the men and women seated on either side of her wore grave expressions on their faces, though she only caught glimpses of them when they thought nobody was looking. She could understand why they were scared. She couldn't understand why any of them were here.

Maybe a sense of duty impelled the others to enter a war zone. Responsibility to Ben was her only motive for being here; she certainly hadn't come for the ambience. And she would rather have thrown herself under the truck's heavy wheels than dodge her responsibilities. So with a dramatic sigh—in case during the past minute Ben had suddenly developed the ability to take a hint—she settled back into the role of accepting what she couldn't change while wishing that she could.

A round of cheers sprang up from a group of soldiers at

the back of the truck, a malevolent presence screaming as if newly born and demanding to be fed. She shivered and huddled closer to Ben.

It can be the brightest day, but fill it with just one dark soul and the day is ruined.

She made a mental note to keep well clear of these soldiers. She hoped Ben was smart enough to do the same.

Finally Ben spoke.

"I'm here to keep my homeland safe," he said.

The tremor in his voice was at odds with his bold statement. She wanted to tell him he could've made trucks at home, but because his eyes were fixed on his boots she succumbed to the rhythm of the back-jarring ride across the pothole-filled road and held her breath, hoping it wouldn't be her last.

Their convoy of flatbed trucks was carrying hundreds of troops, weapons, ammunition, Abrams tanks, armored personnel carriers, and Humvees to the compound, their base for the next six months. With any luck they'd move out faster than they were moving in. Their convoy was doing twenty miles an hour, but she felt as if ants could have passed them.

She wanted to laugh as she pictured tiny insects kicking up orange dust, flipping the bird at the drivers and shouting obscenities. Instead, she bit her lower lip. This was neither the time nor the place to flaunt her eternal optimism. Besides, she wasn't entirely sure she had any cheerfulness left in her.

"I still don't see why we're here," she mumbled.

What made the trip seem slower, she realized, was the lack of perspective. Much like an ocean without any land mass to help judge distance, this desert seemed to stretch endlessly ahead of them. If only the drivers would go faster;

it had to be harder to hit a quicker-moving target. She was tempted to grab Ben by the collar and pull him off the truck, but the heat was around a hundred degrees, and with all the gear packed on them—M-247, M-249, backpack, flak jacket, radio, helmet, goggles — it would've been like sprinting around inside an oven.

Sand began to whirl in all directions, marching up and down the convoy as if sizing it up to establish whether it could be swallowed whole. This was the most dangerous time for the convoy. The trucks had to slow to a crawl or risk running into each other or off the road. Their only saving grace was that the enemy was exposed to the same elements. So while the soldiers couldn't see a thing, they also couldn't be seen. At least that was her hope filled theory.

Time continued to crawl so that after thirty minutes, and since the convoy of soldiers hadn't been killed by unseen enemy fire, she and everyone else began to relax and make conversation.

Their chatter came to a halt when the flatbed truck passed a burned-out tank on the side of the road. Everyone stared open-mouthed at the wreck. Nobody could speak. Nobody could look away.

Despite wanting to peel her eyes away out of respect, she was as enthralled as the rest of them.

She wondered if everyone wanted to know the same thing she did. Had the tank internally combusted from the constant battering of the sun? Nice concept, she thought, but this damage had been caused by man. Judging by the looks on their faces, everyone knew this was the case, and when the eyes of the soldiers around her hardened she guessed they had silently asked another question.

Was this one of their tanks or the enemy's?

They lowered their eyes and turned their heads away,

providing her with the unspoken answer.

"Do you think they got out before it got hit?" she asked Ben.

He didn't respond, but from the rear of the truck one of the loud-mouthed soldiers yelled, "Oh yeah, you're gonna get it now, you freakin' sons of bitches."

A round of cheers followed. Even if she'd known what insults to hurl at these soldiers to quiet them down, she reminded herself that she'd sworn moments ago to steer clear of these men. So she kept her gaze forward and her mouth shut.

Like a good soldier.

A ripple of self-loathing rose and lodged in her throat. She'd never have guessed it would taste so foul.

Outside, the sand was swirling, picking up speed as though being thrown about by a crèche load of bad-tempered toddlers, and pretty soon both the ground and sky were painted flame orange, crackling like an open fire. She was afraid to breathe. Soldiers pulled down their goggles to cover their eyes, but this action was a useless defense against the sand that bit into their exposed flesh.

And still the convoy crawled toward their destination.

The dust finally cleared and the convoy came to a stop outside a large concrete compound that was a series of buildings within four cement walls. Without a word, she and everyone else began unloading the contents of the flatbed trucks—smaller trucks, enough guns to keep the war going for centuries, tanks, food, water and whatever other supplies they'd need for the next six months.

Breathing was difficult. This was the most physical work she'd performed in ages. When she stopped for a break, resentment at the lies welled inside her. Tears stung her eyes.

"Forget home sweet home," she complained silently, "this place is home *sweat* home."

Each and every soldier was drenched from top to bottom from the exertion of working under the glaring sun. Their sweat filled the air; she could have sworn she was in a sauna. Optimism dripped off her forehead. She wiped at her brow and was surprised when her hand came away wet, not with sweat but something else.

No tears. I will not cry.

At least she would not spill tears for herself when others deserved them so much more.

After half an hour, a few companies got into the smaller trucks and disappeared, perhaps to do their hard labor in another section of the growing heat. Another hour after that, once everything had been unloaded, the company she and Ben were assigned to was ordered into one of the smaller trucks, and they too left.

A sergeant with silver hair and eyes was seated in the front. He looked the type who was too mean to have ever had a pet. For long.

"You pussies will stand guard at the hospital for the next twenty-four hours," the sergeant bellowed. "You will each do two twelve-hour shifts, one shift inside the hospital, one outside."

"When do we get time to shoot the enemy?" the kid next to Ben asked. For one so young his eyes were hard, like steel.

"Don't be fooled. The enemy is out there." The sergeant's gravelly voice roared as loudly as the aircraft parading over their heads. "If you ladies find yourself in a threatening situation, well, you know what to do. Are you pussies prepared to protect your fellow countrymen?"

A roar of cheers engulfed the truck. The sound clutched at her heart. If the enemy hadn't known they were here before, they were well aware of it now.

She wanted to reach for Ben's hand and hold it tight, but fear kept her immobile.

"Shoot first and ask questions later. That's what he means," the kid next to Ben said, inching his way closer. "You ever shot a bear? They come at you even after you've pumped ten rounds in 'em. I've heard it's the same with these bastards. You shoot 'em and shoot 'em, but they keep coming at you with guns and knives. All the while cursing at you in the Devil's language. You got to be careful not to touch 'em either. Their blood is poison."

"I doubt we'll shoot anyone at a hospital," Ben replied with a scowl. He moved along the bench as best as he could without falling off the edge. The kid must have gotten the hint because he kept quiet after that.

Unaffected by the searing heat outside, the truck chugged along until it rolled up outside a hospital that had weathered grenade blasts and gunfire till it resembled a thousand-year-old relic.

For some, this was their first time on foreign soil. For others, this was simply another day at work. Yet everyone jumped off the truck and danced boxer-like on their feet as though something invisible was going to jump out from the air and snatch them.

The sky above was on the go with Apache helicopters, hellfire missiles, dust, and jet stream. On the ground was a different story. The air barely stirred. No sign of anyone or anything with a pulse let alone the dreaded enemy. Aside from one or two civilians she could see sneaking peeks at the soldiers from around corners of shattered buildings, the street was empty.

So why could she feel the distinct presence of something out there? Watching, waiting, and blistering with hatred at this invasion.

"Each and every one of you signed a contract with the U.S. Army, which means your asses belong to me," shouted the sergeant.

His eyes scanned the soldiers with no more than a passing glance, as though he already considered them obsolete.

"Your mommies can't help you now. So if any of you pussies don't want to be here, you can kiss my red, white, and blue behind. Now secure the building and welcome to hell."

Chapter One

The DANGER sign was normally enough to keep Jet away.

Not tonight.

She peered into roiling seas below, seeing only moonlight dancing on the waves trapped in the Warriewood blowhole. She'd never been so close before. Usually she watched the crashing waves from the safety of the road, fifty feet above, where cautionary signage warned the unwary of slippery rocks and certain death.

She stood with her back against the cliff, bare feet gripping the slick ledge while sweaty hands clung to the rope tied there by thrill seekers or, perhaps, potential suicides. When the waves flicked up and turned, diving toward the rocks, they cracked as loud as gunfire, but she didn't flinch or loosen her grip. Instead, she closed her eyes and waited, like a lover bracing for a kiss.

A wave shot up, slapping cold, wet fingers against her cheek.

"I guess I deserved that," she whispered, as was her habit to talk to herself when she needed counsel and there was nobody around to provide it.

She swiped at the salt water stinging her cheeks, laughing until she remembered her mission. What was funny about contemplating her final dive?

Waves came in sets of seven, building up in strength each

time. She wiped the salty water from her eyes and returned to staring into the blowhole. What if the next set carried the wave strong enough to take her? Would she sink into the abyss below and disappear into a world where breathing underwater was necessary? God, she hoped so. And not because she wanted to be a mermaid.

Not that she'd ever get to be anything whether actress, singer, or flight attendant. All her dreams were shattered, thanks to Lucas.

Gazing up to a sky filled with pinpricks of twinkling light, she whispered, "Star light, star bright, tell me what to do."

Sometimes the little voice in her head gave her advice, but not this time. Or maybe the pearls of wisdom were silenced by the frantic beating of her heart, banging against her eardrums.

The sea offered no resolution, but continued to dance, aloof and beautiful under an audience of stars. All that was necessary for her to join the dance was to let go of the worn rope. Maybe fate would creep in with the tide and make the decision for her. Maybe the slow scrape of rock against rope would part the aging strands. But the rope was strong. It wouldn't break. The decision was hers and hers alone

She might have let go, and falling might or might not have made her happy, but she never got the chance to find out. Up above, a car door slammed and a cackle of voices broke the solitude. No longer able to spend time alone with her humiliation, she climbed the cliff—itself a risky operation—and headed home.

The house was dark and quiet. As she opened the front gate, she shook off the grim fantasy that the house was waiting to swallow her whole. At least her parents were still out, which was one small blessing. Their absence left her with a few hours to mentally prepare for the verbal thrashing she was about to cop.

"No matter what, I'll never be ready to face them," she said as she walked along the path.

Disillusionment stabbed deep within in her chest as she jammed the key into the lock on the front door. She let out a loud grunt when it wouldn't turn.

"Stupid lock. What's wrong with you?"

After fighting with the lock for another few minutes, she figured it'd been changed or bolted from the inside while she was out so she squeezed past azaleas and hydrangeas on her way around the side of the house where she slid the window frame to the bathroom window and shimmied her way inside the house.

When she landed on the tiled floor, she kicked over the laundry hamper. She stubbed her toe on the vanity so she sent a stray sock hurling through the air in retaliation.

Her lips quivered, and she gulped back on a fresh bout of tears. "God damn it! Surely they're meant to be there for better or worse."

Even overlooking the fact that she was confusing wedding vows with parental responsibility, she had a point. They were her parents. If ever a time existed to remind them of their duty to fix or forgive her mistakes, now was as good as any.

But she was getting ahead of herself. Maybe they wouldn't find out her terrible secret. Maybe they wouldn't kill her. Maybe her worries were all for nothing.

She climbed up the stairs to her bedroom (if it was still her room. For all she knew her parents were checking out pet stores to buy something bred for obedience) and made herself a pledge.

"If I have a text message I'll do it," she whispered. "If I

don't… Well, we'll see."

A game of chance to be letting a cell phone decide my fate, she thought. But she saw no other choice. And while switching off her phone or throwing it out the window seemed like the two best options, both were social suicide. Instead, she hurried up the stairs and scanned for messages, finding eight. None were what she'd call pleasant.

No backing out now. A promise is a promise.

Rummaging through her parents' closet produced two bottles. One contained vodka, the other sleeping pills. She unscrewed the caps to both and sat on her bed.

No backing out of what?

Drinking herself into oblivion? She was hardly an expert on the subject. What few friends she had were as apprehensive of drugs and alcohol as she was. Correction. As apprehensive as she used to be. She touched the vodka bottle to her lips and took a tentative sip, the hard glass rim clattering against her teeth. As the hot liquid burned her stomach she reminded herself that she had made a silent pledge.

No backing out. No backing out.

It became a chant as she swallowed large mouthfuls. Her belly churned as the vodka hit.

Get a grip. Not like this is your first time at getting wasted.

Her hold on the bottle faltered.

First times always had an unrealistic emphasis placed on them. The first bicycle. The first kiss. The first warm rush as alcohol hits the blood stream, bringing sense from the senseless.

The first sexual encounter…

She bit the bottle's rim, taking gulp after gulp, and everything began to make sense. She had to go through with this; she couldn't live a second longer with the humiliation.

She took a break from drinking herself into oblivion only to hit the stereo's remote control. Cranking out of the speakers was her favorite artist, Pink. She loved the music so much she'd decorated her room in as many shades of pink as she could find. Fuchsia. Magenta. Candy. Even salmon made it into the ensemble by way of a throw rug. Usually Pink's hard-hitting lyrics did the trick, channeling her sour mood to something else. Her stuffed toys mostly. Not this time.

"Don't hate me, Teddy," she whispered, picking up her favorite toy and jamming her face into his soft belly.

Then, hit with a fresh wave of humiliation, she shoved the stuffed animal under the pillow so it couldn't witness, or judge, her behavior.

Her chest burned from vodka, and shame pierced her insides. Despite having cried for days already, more sobs shook her. A calmer part of her wondered how she had more tears left to shed. Yet she wept from a hidden reservoir stashed deep inside her. Though her stomach heaved and begged "no more" she continued to guzzle vodka. Three-quarters through the bottle, she opened the container containing her mom's sleeping pills, which she then tossed down like M&M's.

As the CD ended, two empty bottles fell to the floor. Less than a second later so did she.

Her fall took her to a place where it was quiet at last.

* * *

Jet woke without any sense of how long her blackout had lasted. Long enough for her to wake up in a room nothing like she imagined a detox clinic would look like. This room resembled a North Queensland holiday resort. Highly unlikely she was so far from home. Her dad might have had a change of heart and coughed up the cash for a recuperating holiday, but a trip to North Queensland required a boarding pass. So unless plane trips were being handed out for free, she was somewhere on the southern side of the Sydney Harbor Bridge. Perhaps Bondi or Coogee. Smiling, she decided she didn't care where she was. She was miles away from home and school and that was all that mattered.

She surveyed the room with interest. The floor and walls were the color of bleached coral. The wood furnishings were pale blond. The sofa and armchairs were covered in a beige-on-beige, striped fabric. Beige looked good in brochures and magazines, she realized, but the "drained of color and life" look was just sad. Only paintings of emerald palm fronds, scarlet hibiscus flowers, and azure water, strikingly bright against the dull neutrals, gave the place any vitality. Perhaps the beige furnishings were designed as a backdrop for the paintings and scenery.

A full-length mirror on the wall marked where the dining room ended and the sitting room began in the open living space. She screwed up nose up at the mirror. How horridly old fashioned, she thought, like something from the Tudor period, with a thick, gold frame and engravings on all four sides that resembled eyes. Possibly of Egyptian origin. The mirror was ugly and out of place. But she was both repulsed and obsessed with it.

She tore her gaze away from the mirror and looked over the rest of the room. A galley kitchen gleamed with white counters and stainless steel appliances. A set of glass sliding doors led to an outside balcony, where young palms in cane planters framed the view of the distant ocean. A big screen TV, its surface blank, was fixed to the wall. These were the sort of things she'd have expected to find in a resort.

There were two things in the room as out of place as the ancient mirror. On the sofa sat a young girl who was sucking on the end of her black ponytail as though it contained hidden calories. And on an armchair next to her was a guy with a broody look on his face.

Jet guessed the girl was a year or so younger and the guy a year or two older. The girl was a chubbier, less stylized version of Jet herself. She'd have considered the girl pretty if the hairs on Jet's nape hadn't lifted in suspicion.

The guy carried the handsome, haunted look well even if his hands and face appeared as if they'd spent too long in the sun. His hair might have been strawberry blond, but his head was closely shaved with only stubble poking out of the top and from his chin. Wearing khaki pants, a grey shirt, and hiking boots, he looked as if he'd be more at home in a desert or a jungle.

She guessed he was a soldier based on his ramrod posture.

"I'm Rachael," said the girl. "This is Ben."

Jet felt Rachael's eyes watching her intently. Jet stared back.

Rachael slipped her hands into her lap and curled them in a ball. "We weren't expecting you, but welcome."

While Rachael seemed surprised to see Jet, a flicker of the eyes was the only sign Ben gave that they were all on the same planet. When Jet followed the trail to where she thought his gaze was fixated on, she found his attention was fixed on the gold-framed mirror.

Was it supposed to be doing something?

Better he's zoned out than to think I've lost my charm, she thought.

"And you are…" Rachael asked.

"Impressed," said Jet. "What is this place?"

"It's a healing center."

Jet wondered if her father would have put her somewhere this flashy if he'd understood why she'd taken an overdose. More likely he'd have stashed her somewhere with tall towers, patrolling ogres and hair plaiting classes.

Rachael shot an odd look in Ben's direction, and Jet picked up on the glance, yet she couldn't tell if the young girl was seeking approval or hiding something. But Jet really didn't care either way, which surprised her. She usually enjoyed gossip and intrigue. Being the brunt of gossip and intrigue had kind of stripped the fascination for it out of her.

"It's nothing like I imagined," Jet said. She did a slow cruise of the room, touching things as she went. Cool, hard, shiny, soft. Everything was real, all right. Frowning, she added, "I also figured it would be a lot more crowded. Are we the only ones here?"

Rachael's gaze didn't lessen in its intensity. "The others are around somewhere."

"I'd better have my own room."

Rachael shrugged her shoulders. "That would be the opposite of constructive. Sorry. You'll have to share a room with me."

She didn't sound too thrilled about having a roommate and jet realized the sentiment was mutual. At least at home, Jet had her own room, at the end of the hallway and far from her parents'. The privacy was the only thing she liked about her home life.

Jet slumped into the empty armchair opposite Ben; he

was still staring at the mirror as if it would magically transform itself into a TV. He didn't move, not even when she began waving her hands in front of her face.

"What's the matter with him?" she asked Rachael.

Rachael's face crumpled in what Jet took as defeat. "He's usually more talkative. But we've just finished Group. I guess he's tired."

"Group?"

Instead of explaining, Rachael reached under the coffee table and pulled out a book the size of a personal diary, which she pushed across the table. "We're supposed to write everything in this journal. Our thoughts, feelings, fears, our name—"

"Julliet Jones. Jet for short."

"—so we can talk about what we've written."

"That's not a rule, is it? I mean, I don't gotta hand this in at the end of the day?"

Rachael shook her head. "Nobody else has to read it. Unless you really want to—"

"I don't really want to."

"—and it would be wrong to snoop—"

"Totally."

"—but you do have to bring something to the session for discussion." Rachael tilted her head and lifted her gaze upwards as if she'd just remembered something. "If you don't mind, I'd like to lead the sessions. Ben is still uncomfortable talking about what happened so we have to watch what we say."

"Can't say I blame him for vagueing out," Jet said. By this time, her mind had left the conversation entirely and she was scanning the room for the TV remote. "Talk is overrated."

"Spoken like someone who has something to hide. Look,

the fastest way out of this place is to heal the mind. And the best way to heal the mind is to be honest with it. And the best way to be honest with the mind is to talk openly, without opinion or judgment, about why we are here."

Rachael's last remark snagged Jet's attention. "What's with this 'we' business? I know why I'm here. Why are you here?"

Instead of answering, Rachael gave a self-satisfied smile. "I asked you first. What is it you believe you need to do to be well again?"

The girl's smugness sat on Jet's skin like a pesky mosquito. Anxious that things be set straight from the beginning, she looked Rachael square in the eye. "I don't have to get well again because there's nothing wrong with me. My father has recognized my cry for attention for what it is and has rewarded me with a vacation."

"A what?" Rachael almost choked on a loud, snorting laugh. "Are you sure you wouldn't prefer Disneyland? Now that's a vacation." She shook her head and took a deep breath. "Sorry. I don't know what's come over me. I'm usually not so—"

"Smug?"

"Irritable."

Rachael pursed her lips and folded her hands in her lap, looking too stiff and formal, like a giant old-fashioned doll. Jet found it creepy.

"Denial slows the healing process," Rachael said. She fixed sapphire eyes on Ben and lowered her voice. "I shouldn't say this, but he acts as though nothing traumatic happened to make him erase six months from his mind."

The hairs on Jet's arms bristled at the way Rachael was talking about Ben like he was invisible, which was generally considered rude and disrespectful. She was about to say something when a thought struck her.

"He's not deaf, is he?"

Rachael shook her head. "No. He just can't remember the war."

"Can't remember, or won't talk? Make up your mind."

Rachael's lips tightened till they were a grim line on her face. "His memory is deeply repressed. Nothing seems to be working to loosen it."

Ben still hadn't acknowledged her, and Jet was becoming cranky. Here she was, sticking up for him while Rachael treated him like a second-class citizen, and he wouldn't even make eye contact with her. Where were her parents so she could demand they place her in a treatment center with well-mannered patients? They should have been here. Surely they wouldn't have waived their rights to lecture her to death.

Come to think of it, she told herself, where were the swarms of doctors and nurses hell-bent on extracting the essence of childhood out of them?

Jet gave her temple a few quick taps with her index finger, driving off the weird feeling that tickled her bones and returned to the conversation. "Maybe he's brain dead. You know, took a piece of shrapnel to the head."

She hoped this wasn't the case. The longer she stared at him, the more she realized that he was even more gorgeous than at first glance. If his hair was to grow out a little and the sunburn was to fade from his face…A niggling feeling in her stomach told her this was neither the time nor the place to reflect on his physical attraction. But how could she look at a rainbow and not admire it?

"He's not brain dead."

Rachael folded her arms across her chest. Maybe she wanted to appear intimidating, but to Jet the girl came across as sulky. Jet's anger softened, until a moment later the smug expression returned to Rachael's face, and she said, "Let's get back to my original question. What brings you here?"

Jet wanted to punch the girl in the face. If self-righteousness was an infectious disease, then Jet vowed to get as far away from Rachael as possible. Maybe Jet wasn't perfect, maybe she had regrets and she'd made mistakes – the biggest mistake had landed her in this place – but she wasn't the type to shoot a reproachful stare at a stranger and expect them to be thankful for the judgment.

Jet stood and pointed at the book still sitting on the table. "Well, as I haven't written anything in my journal, I can't participate in Group, can I? So I'll go and see if this place has a pool."

Chapter Two

To say that Rachael had been surprised to see Jet standing in the room was an understatement. At the sight of the young woman, panic had filled her. This place wasn't big on fanfares but a newcomer to the group seemed like something she should have known about.

"I wonder why she's here," she whispered. She shook her head in amazement as Jet disappeared down the hallway in search of a pool as though this place was a resort. "Can you believe her? A pool."

"Are you jealous?" Ben asked.

Rachael bit her lip. How much of the conversation had Ben heard? She realized she'd need to choose her words carefully from now on. Or stop thinking out loud.

"Of course not," she said. "Why would you even suggest it? I just don't like change. It disrupts things."

"Change is meant to be good. You know, a sign of progress." Ben's smile suggested he was teasing her.

She rarely liked to be teased but it was almost worth it to see him smile.

"Change isn't about progress," she said. "It's about keeping the wheels of commercialism and capitalism turning so there's continual economic growth, which, by the way, is spinning humanity out of control. Change brings nothing but setbacks."

She shook her head while lifting her chin in stalwart

resolution.

Ben rewarded her outburst with silence.

"Besides," she added sulkily, "we were doing fine, just the two of us."

His shrill laugh sent icicles though her veins. "Speak for yourself. I think even you have to admit I haven't been doing so well."

Her smile faltered. Negativity was more dangerous than change. Negativity was a force like a vortex with a habit of drawing anyone nearby into it.

I am an eternal source of optimism.

She lifted her cheeks into a huge smile, though using those muscles hurt so much. Before, when only the two of them mattered, it had been perfectly fine to walk around all day with a sour face.

"You need a change of perspective," she said. "Maybe we should watch DVDs and make comparisons with our lives against the struggles the heroes are facing."

He shrugged his shoulders. "Nah. And why are you talking like the *TV Guide*?"

She scowled, ignoring his attempts to change the subject. "We could watch *Saving Private Ryan*. Isn't that your favorite movie?"

"You know I have trouble remembering stuff like that."

"*Full Metal Jacket*?"

Ben shook his head.

"*Starship Troopers*? *Predator*? *South Pacific*?"

He shot her an exasperated look. "Rach. Watching a bunch of people get blown to bits seems to me the least likely way of unlocking repressed memories."

"It's just a thought." She paused, pursing her lips. "Ben, I want you to be happy. Please try it. Doctors say positive thinking is the most powerful method of healing of them all."

"Maybe the doctors you've seen," he mumbled under his breath.

She clenched her fists. Boy, she wanted to hit him on the head. With something heavy, too, heavy enough to crack open his skull and set his deepest memories free because his forgetfulness was becoming more and more frustrating with each new dawn. Especially when she was sure his memories were on the verge of spilling out like a flood. And he seemed to be the only thing holding back the flow.

"I just think she's the type trouble follows," Rachael said. "I'm entitled to my opinion, aren't I?"

She unclenched her fists, the blood draining away until her fingers were bone white. Her vision glistened as her eyes filled with tears. She squeezed them shut to stem the flow. She knew why she was upset at this newcomer's presence here; she just didn't want to admit it to herself. She was jealous.

Ben gave a gentle laugh. "You're jealous."

If only loving him didn't hurt so much, then she wouldn't have these crazy, and unfamiliar feelings running around insider her, causing her mind and her heart to question why each of them was here.

"I'm only watching out for you," she whispered. "Is that a crime?"

She opened her eyes in time to see his face cloud as if shadowed. Why it clouded, she didn't know. But it did.

"I don't need you to look after me." He stood and stormed over to the mirror, then put his forehead on the glass and closed his eyes. When she thought he was never going to speak to her again, he whirled and shook a clenched fist at her. "I don't need you or anyone else to look after me."

She didn't flinch. Ben would never hurt her.

"You're in a rotten mood today," she muttered under her breath.

He could barely remember his name some days, and now he was declaring his independence.

She closed her eyes. *I am an ocean of wellness in mind, body, and spirit.*

"At least she's pretty."

Her back stiffened. Comfort had made her forget just how perceptive he could be. At least there was nothing wrong with that part of his brain. Still, his comment about Jet's attractiveness hit a nerve. Already exhausted from Group, Rachael's eyes again began to tear up.

Ben crossed the space between them in one stride. When he sat, he winked at her. "But not as pretty as you."

"You're a jerk." She was laughing as she threw a cushion at his head. She never could stay mad at him.

Jet broadcasted her return to the room with a loud slam of the door. "What's so funny? By the way, this place sucks." She leaped into the armchair and swung her feet onto the coffee table. "I mean, there's a pool on the roof but the gate is locked. Whose stupid idea was it to do that? What are we supposed to do till it opens?"

"Why would there be a pool on the roof?" Ben asked, curiosity crinkling his face.

"At last, Soldier Boy is awake. Good, because I'm starved. When do we eat around here?" Jet swiveled her neck as if searching for something, scowling when she couldn't find what she wanted. "What *is* the time?"

"A hair past a freckle but the freckle's catching up," Ben said, grinning.

It was such a stupid, simple thing for Ben to say, something from his childhood, but Jet's eyes lit and

Rachael's eyes tightened with worry. Reason told her the new girl was no threat, but the soft twinkle in Jet's blue eyes that gripped at Rachael's stomach told her otherwise. And now Ben had the same pathetic twinkle in his eyes.

"We'll eat soon," Rachael said. "And we get to eat whatever we want. Isn't that right, Ben? We can have hamburgers, hot dogs, pizza."

He shrugged. "Been a while since I had a good slice of pizza."

"So what do we do till we eat?" Jet waved a finger at Rachael. "And don't tell me we sit around here talking about our feelings, because I'm not interested."

"Talking is pretty much all we do. It helps us to figure out how to get better." Rachael bit her lip and wrung her hands together.

"Jesus, you never give up, do you? What a waste of time your psychobabble sessions are. Look at this place, it's amazing."

Ben sat up. "I wouldn't go that far. Anyway, what sort of things are you interested in?"

Jet leaned across the coffee table. She flicked black hair off her shoulders and tilted her head to the side. "I'm interested in all kinds of things. Like you. Are you here on vacation?"

Ben seemed to be drawn by her attraction. He leaned over the coffee table until his head was inches away from hers. As though an invisible shield surrounded the two of them, Rachael felt as if her body was being pushed by this invisible shield deep into the sofa.

Ben's eyes had a dreamy hue to them. His upper lip twitched as though hiding a smile. "My memory isn't so great. How about you tell me why I'm here?"

"Well, you're an American soldier, so I'm guessing your

plane got shot down over the Pacific Ocean, you have amnesia, and now you're stuck until you can figure out how to get home."

"Now that you're here, maybe I don't wanna go home."

Rachael put her hands on her face. She wanted to scream and cry at the same time. She was right about Jet bringing trouble to the group. It had followed her in and had set something off inside Ben that was the biological equivalent of Superglue.

Chapter Three

Ben had lied when he'd said Jet was pretty. She was hot. And she had an awesome smile, the kind that could blindside you. Maybe it was or wasn't love at first sight, but Jet's smile filled the hole in his heart and for a brief moment he didn't care that nothing could fill the deep well in his head.

Rachael didn't laugh the way Jet was laughing. Jet's joy seemed to erupt from deep within, and her eyes glowed like rare gemstones. Even sapphires weren't so vibrant. His mom had once told him that blue gemstones promoted peace. Was this why he could have listened to the soothing melody of Jet's voice forever?

Maybe he was besotted with her Australian accent. He'd met a few Aussies in the army. Always telling tall stories and coming across as jokers the way they dropped vowels off words to make fewer syllables. Those Aussies sure travelled around a lot, he thought with a chuckle. They were everywhere these days.

Still, he figured he must look like a schmuck, nodding his head and hanging onto her every word, but at least while she was chattering away, a clear space sat on the spot inside his head that was usually cluttered with the ashes of bad dreams.

His inner asylum didn't last long. Jet said something about hating to have her hair cut, and the little bug inside his head clocked on. It began tunneling down toward the cluttered part of his brain. There, it sifted through rubble and held up a memory of the time he'd enlisted in the army. He'd come home wearing a combat uniform and with all his hair shaved clean off. His mom had gotten so upset she'd run out of the house screaming. It had annoyed him at the time. Joining the army was the one thing he'd done for himself, and she'd carried on as if he'd eloped with his cousin.

The little bug scurried off again to sort through another pile of junk and this time it found a memory from a few months before he'd enlisted. On the fridge was a yellow note with DINNER IN OVEN written on it. Like all of his mom's notes, it hadn't meant what was written on it. She'd once written OFF TO WORK NOW, forgetting that she hadn't worked at the motel for over a year. Still, he'd checked the oven to be sure, only instead of his dinner cooking in the oven, he'd found his sneakers simmering away, shrunk to half their size. At the time she'd blamed a head cold for muddling up her brain, and Ben had believed her because his mother never lied.

His bringing home a pretty girl would be something to occupy his mom's mind, he thought. She would be as fascinated with Jet as he was. She could get caught up in planning a wedding and christening and birthday parties. Even if nothing more than the planning kept her busy, at least it would be something.

Ben shifted his attention the way a car shifts gears— down, up, a little to the right, up or down again. He admired the way Jet was sitting on the armchair. It had nothing to do with the way the sleeve of her T-shirt slipped off her shoulder and exposed a trio of beauty marks. It had to do with the way she was blocking the images he saw in the mirror.

No, not quite images actually, but floaty things passing in and out of his vision, enough that he wondered if the mirror was haunted. Stupid really. He should take Rachael's advice and not look. But he'd become addicted to staring, and the more he told himself not to, the more he couldn't stop.

Rachael said residue from the spray cleaner made the glass appear milky. But that couldn't be right. His mom never used commercial cleaners. She was old-school, mixing vinegar with water. Her solution left the glass top of the dining table so clean...

Frowning, Ben stood up. Something was wrong with the layout of the room. His face drained of color as realization hit him with a sharp slap. "Who moved the table?"

Chapter Four

Jet was halfway through telling Ben the story of how she'd almost become a back-up singer in a band, but had bailed out at the last minute because the band had scored a gig interstate and she was hardly ever allowed outside her own yard, when he stood up and brushed past her as he headed to the other side of the room. And he went with such a purposeful stride that for a second she thought as if he was going to jump off the balcony.

"What are you doing?" she asked, startled.

He began pulling the chairs out from under the dining table. "The setting's got to be moved."

The table seemed perfectly fine aligned, set dead center of the two glass sliding doors that overlooked the outside world. "Where is it supposed to be?"

He showed her where by pushing and pulling at the table and chairs till they were pressed up hard against the wall.

Jet scowled. The symmetry was destroyed. "Put it back where it belongs."

"It belongs here."

"But you're blocking the way out to the balcony."

"Mom can't find the furniture in the wrong spot."

"Are you out of your mind?" Jet hit her forehead with her hand in mock surprise. "Well, of course you are. You took a piece of shrapnel to the head."

When Ben turned around to face her, his vacant stare sent

a shiver up her spine. She realized he wasn't even looking at her. His eyes were locked on something behind her.

"Rachael, tell Jet what happened the last time furniture was moved around." Ben's eyes pleaded with the young girl to agree with what he was saying.

"Sorry. I don't remember." Rachael kept her eyes fixed firmly on the floor.

"Of course you remember." Ben's face was turning red. "Mom called the cops. She thought someone had broken into the house."

* * *

Within seconds the living area had become as uncomfortable as the one at home, so Jet got up and wedged herself between the wall and the dining table. The wind had died down so the potted palms on the balcony weren't slapping across the glass sliding doors, but dancing lazily from side to side. Her journal sat open in front of her, ready and waiting for her mind to leap onto the pages. So far, all she could manage was her name. Off to a good start, she told herself. Albeit a bit like writing your name at the top of the school exam was a good start.

She'd read somewhere that clouds could act like a valve to release creative juices, and if you stared at them long enough the juices would flow. But after an hour she had to admit that her strengths lay elsewhere. The clouds were still clouds and she was no closer to cataloguing her thoughts than when she'd first opened her journal. Indeed, the effort of trying to write, coupled with the heat streaming in through the glass, was making her drowsy. So she rested her head against the wall and tears stung her eyes as an unwanted memory from a few weeks ago floated up to the surface.

"Well, I'm heading overseas again tomorrow," Jet's father had announced right before he'd plunged his fork into a pile of mashed potatoes.

"Another business trip?" Jet pushed her plate away. "I haven't even left the state. If it wasn't for that field trip in Grade Three I'd never have seen the Opera House."

"Why would you want to go anywhere?"

Because I'm fed up with prisoners getting treated better than me, she wanted to say but didn't dare.

Every other person on the planet enjoyed traveling. Not her dad. He carried on as if his business trips were the ones where you woke up in a bathtub full of ice minus a kidney. Years ago she'd grown bored of pretending to complain, but not playing his game only made dinner conversation all the more uninteresting so she'd kept it up. Lately she was only pretending to pretend-complain about not going anywhere because Lucas, the boyfriend her father was clueless about, was talking about whisking her away for a romantic weekend.

Sometimes Jet was bursting to tell her father she had a boyfriend. If only to add some chaotic glitter to his perfectly orchestrated life.

He stared at her over the rim of his glasses, making her feel smaller than usual. Even the overcooked vegetables were begging to be released from his heavy scrutiny.

"It's a business trip," he said. "And the day the Government decides it's permissible to use taxpayers' money to take family vacations is the day you'll get to come with me."

She caught her mother's nervous-yet-blistering smile. Jet could tell what her mom was thinking; she'd contemplated it herself often enough. Dad earned a fortune but spent none of it on his family. What clothes her mother managed to sneak into the house had to be washed ten times to resemble something that looked as if it had lived in the closet for years. Jet had to hide the expensive clothes that Lucas had given her under her mattress, and found that undignified.

For Christ's sake this isn't the Sixties, she'd internally screamed as her grip tightened on the fork. The women in this house were supposed to have rights.

"Where are you going this time?" Jet gave a dramatic sigh. "Paris. Milan. London. I hear they have the most beautiful dresses overseas."

Her mother glared at her. Jet glared back. She was still angry at her mother's refusal to buy her the red, backless dress she'd wanted to wear to her end of year formal dance.

"I hear you get dresses overseas for half the price we pay here." Jet kept her eyes level with her mother in defiance. "That's because you avoid paying the shipping and retailer markup costs."

What did he care how much a dress cost? Surely his daughter's happiness was more important. Maybe she should have just come right out and asked him for it.

She quickly discarded this thought when she saw her mother's face and neck had turned purple.

Her father took off his glasses. "Now, Julliet. How about you concentrate on your studies and forget what you see in fashion magazines? Anyway, the trip's nothing exciting. I'm off to Jakarta for a very boring conference." He put his glasses back on and returned to sawing through the overcooked chop with a butter knife.

While we sit around here like dogs waiting for you to

throw us your scraps, she thought, but her mother was choking on her fruit juice so Jet was spared from saying anything further.

* * *

Jet wasn't aware she'd fallen asleep at the dining table until she was jolted awake by something hitting the balcony door, which turned out to be a palm frond. She was certain something more sinister had caused her stuttering heartbeat; she couldn't shake the feeling a fist had knocked on the glass door.

She was alone. Ben and Rachael must have left the room while she'd dozed off. She was used to loneliness, but at home or school some kind of background noise usually could be heard. A gang of mimes would have been welcomed in this unsettling silence. Still, she found the surprising quiet soothing, so she returned to staring across the ocean as another thought spread throughout her, this one so new to her she wondered if it came with a warranty.

She was being encouraged to speak her mind after spending years living as a scripted player under her father's direction.

Should she write anything at all? What if the journal was handed over to her parents? They'd read it for sure. Trust was a big issue in the Jones household.

While her journal sat open on the dining table, naked and without a single word to mar the page, millions of phrases danced around inside her head. Twice she'd picked up the pen to write down her ideas, inspirations, and opinions. And twice she'd decided against it.

One strong emotion resonated in her pondering.

She missed her mother.

Sighing, she wished she could conjure up her the loving power of her mom the way Ben apparently could. Maybe time was the key. If so, she had all the time in the world, because as much as she hated this eerie healing center, she was in no hurry to go home either.

Without a sound, Ben entered the room. One second he wasn't there and the next he was. Then he followed a path that went from the start of the room to the end as though on autopilot, and he seemed to sidestep invisible obstacles as he marched left, right, left across the living room till he got to his armchair. Jet was about to say hello when she realized he hadn't noticed her at all. He was staring at the mirror with a puzzled expression distorting his handsome features.

"Ben," she called out to him, simply to get his face to return to normal.

The mirror's hold on him was broken, and he shot her a sheepish grin. "Hey. Sorry about freaking out earlier. Turns out the dining setting was fine where it was. I'll move it back if you want."

"No, it's okay." Out over the balcony railing, she could see boats bobbing up and down on the water. "Are we having Group today?"

Ben shrugged his shoulders. "Suppose so."

"It's just that I haven't written much in my journal. I don't know what to write either."

"Ask Rachael. She's good with that sort of thing."

"What would she know? She's just a kid." Jet was surprised at the amount of venom in her voice.

"But she's a good kid."

"So you agree she's just a kid?"

Ben gave her an odd look and she wondered why she

was jealous of Rachael. Maybe because she remembered her own behavior at that age. Her hormones had kicked in, and she'd gone from hating boys one second to wondering where they'd been all her life the next. Besides, she didn't need to be jealous of Rachael. She hadn't mistaken the sparks that had showered off Ben yesterday and landed on her. They had connected, even if this blazing flash of connectivity was the same spark that had triggered his brain into running of its rails, much like Frankenstein's monster had run off the rails when electricity was zapped into his flesh. Still, Ben seemed to have returned to the land of the normal, and the chemistry that hung in the air vibrated like a thousand bees rushing toward a solitary flower.

"Where did you live before you went to war?" she asked. "Or don't you remember?"

He laughed. "Now that's something I'll never forget. I grew up in a small town in Idaho."

"What's it like, this small town in Idaho?"

"Nice."

Convinced she was never going to be a writer, Jet closed her journal and went to the sofa. "Nice, because it has year-round sunshine and no school? Nice, because it's a place where adults are banned and you can eat all the ice cream you want? Come on, you gotta give me more than 'nice'."

She sensed Ben was the quiet type, yet she hoped he'd open up to her. Besides a need to find out what he was like as a person, she was infatuated by his American accent. Hearing the accent on TV was not the same as hearing it in real life. She found it incredibly sexy.

He leaned back into the chair. "I was born and raised in a town called Riggins. It's a narrow town that lies in between two deep gorges and on the banks of two rivers. A good place to live I suppose. People care about each other. My dad used to say you could only call a place home if you considered your neighbor as your brother, and not just the guy who lived next door. My dad used to say a lot of wise things."

She'd picked up on the past tense. "Used to?"

"He died a few years back. When he was alive we lived on acreage on Squaw Creek. Afterwards, we moved to a small house on Main Street. That's why I do a lot of camping, fishing, hunting and hiking. I need to be outdoors."

"You go hunting? With a gun?"

He nodded. "And knives. Bows and arrows sometimes. Traps occasionally, but girls get squeamish when they hear talk of trapping an animal."

Jet scrunched up her nose. She'd never met a guy like him before. Lucas was into animal rights and had habitually lectured her on things like propaganda that spanned the globe, anarchy that was happening in her own backyard, and other newsworthy topics, which she found dull. He'd even tried to convert her to vegetarianism, despite her suspicions that the burger wrappers in his car belonged to him and not his mates, as he so often claimed. Small wonder she was fascinated by how Ben could treat the things Lucas hated as typical weekend activities.

"Have you shot and killed anything?" she asked and instantly regretted asking it. "Whoa. Forget I just said that. You're obviously traumatized by the war."

Ben nestled his body deeper into the sofa. "It's all right. I enjoy talking about home. Things are normal there."

Jet gave him a fierce look. "Killing animals for fun is normal?"

He laughed and held up his hands in mock defeat. "Hey, don't get mad. Girls hunt for bargains. Guys hunt for food.

What's the difference?"

"Well, for a start, I don't go shopping."

"A girl who doesn't shop? I don't believe it."

"Well, you'd better believe it. However, it's not because I don't want to." She shrugged her shoulders but the bitter mood was adamant that it wanted to settle there. "You need money to go shopping."

He nodded in understanding. "Yeah, I know what you mean. There's not a lot of money in our house either."

"Oh, lack of money isn't what's stopping me. My dad's rich, he's just a total scrooge. I reckon he keeps Mom and me poor so we can't escape."

Ben sighed. "Sometimes more trouble comes from escaping than staying."

"Well, lucky I ended up here then, because I have no intentions of leaving."

Jet heard a groan behind her and bristled.

Freakin' Rachael eavesdropping, I'll bet, she told herself.

She turned her head but saw no one else in the room.

Chapter Five

Rachael swished her way into the room the next morning, waving her journal high into the air.

"Time for Group."

Now there were three of them in Group, she considered putting bells on her journal. Rules were rules. No writing or reading in another person's journal without the other person's express permission, even if this was a rule she'd created. She actually had no objections to Ben nosing around into her book of deepest, darkest musings, but she was unable and unwilling to trust Jet.

Jet absently ran her fingers through her hair. "Do we have to? I haven't written a thing."

A niggle of doubt ran through Rachael at the girl's lack of participation, but Rachael kept her smile in check. She'd already made up her mind that Jet had brought trouble to the group. But when Ben had revealed yesterday he wasn't doing so well, that had almost floored her. If these two pooled their skepticism together she'd be done for. Group was all she had.

Rachael sweetened her smile and spoke as if she was talking to a child. "Of course we have to. Why else are we here?"

"But where are the others?" Jet asked, looking around and even taking a quick peek under the coffee table. "It can't be just the three of us. This is the oddest Group therapy I've ever heard about, only three people. That's not a group, it's a clique."

"Are you hoping to hide among a bigger crowd?" asked Rachael, hating the way her voice sounded snooty. "Well, if you think hiding will get you out of confronting your inner demons, you're mistaken."

Besides, a large group of people was the last thing Rachael wanted. She'd found the sessions hard enough to handle when she was alone with Ben.

She waved her hand through the air. "I suppose the others are around somewhere. You can track them down if you want. I couldn't be bothered. So, who wants to go first?"

"I'm not ready to participate," Jet said. "And I doubt you're qualified to hold a therapy session."

Rachael's neck and back burned as if Jet's skepticism had leaped off her and taken up root there. Her foot twitched as though preparing to stomp up and down in frustration. She pleaded with her brain to stay still. Any display would only make her appear childish, and she already suspected these two saw her as a kid.

One day Jet would understand how important these sessions were, she reasoned. Until then, Rachael was only too happy to remind her.

"Money can buy a lot of things but it can't buy doctors twenty-four-seven," she explained. "Anyway, I've been here so long they should just give me a white coat and a clipboard."

"She does know the lingo," Ben said.

Jet's challenging glare broke Rachael's resolve. She let out a sigh and said, "You're right. I'm not qualified. But it wouldn't hurt you to tell us what's on your mind. You've worn through the glass with staring at it so much."

"I was thinking how my problems—not that I have any—

are nobody's business. Least of all yours."

Rachael looked away. "Suit yourself. What about you, Ben? Do you have something you wish to share?"

At least he appeared to be avoiding the rebellious stare Jet flicked his way as he paged through his journal, though his eyes often wavered from the book in his lap to the mirror on the wall.

Was she losing him? She would do everything to stop that from happening. Yet he seemed to be even more withdrawn lately. Watching him wrestle with the floodgates holding in his memories was becoming too painful to bear. She ached to reach out a hand and stroke his cheek, though physical contact was forbidden.

She decided the best thing she could do for him was to sit still and display the virtue of patience while he flipped through page after page. This simple act was worse than watching a kettle boil. Her hand begged to reach out and grab the book, while her mouth yearned to yell at him to damned well read whatever page he found.

At last, he got to near the end of his book, yet his lips were twisted like he was being forced to do this against his will. In a way he was, but Rachael held her breath, worried he was going to put the book on the coffee table and storm off.

His features softened, and he leaned his head back into the sofa. He was almost hidden behind his book as he read aloud:

"I wake up each day knowing there are numbers I'm supposed to remember. Like the number of days I've sat on this couch. It feels like years but it must only be a few months. Another day has been added, yet I feel no different to what I felt yesterday.

"I'm supposed to remember the number of lives I've

taken for my head to hurt so much that a red, blistery scar has soldered itself over my memory. Am I also supposed to remember the number of times I've asked forgiveness for something I can't remember doing in the first place?

"I want to be rid of the shame that eats at me like rats gnawing on electrical cables. Dawn till dusk, my spirit is breaking. Getting smashed like bananas beneath heavy boots. Dusk till dawn, my soul is rotting. Decayed like the faceless enemy who plagues my dreams and will till the day I die—"

"Stop!" Jet stood up and covered her ears with her hands. "Just stop. No wonder you're miserable. That's horrible. Morbid. Depressing. And to think I used to like it when men bared their soul. Enough!"

Rachael shot Jet an angry stare. So did Ben.

He forced his next words out through clenched teeth. "You have no idea what I went through."

"Maybe not. But it's a beautiful day outside and you're sitting here reading suicide letters." Jet swatted the journal out of his hands and pulled him out of the chair. "Come on. What you need is less Group and more Fun. Let's go for a swim."

He allowed himself to be dragged along, but glanced at Rachael as though seeking approval. She smiled inwardly that she had not totally lost her grip on his friendship.

Jet glared at Rachael first, then at Ben. "She's not your keeper, Ben. You can make up your own mind."

"He should stay here." Rachael had found a sudden boost in her confidence. As long as she retained control she could undo the damage Jet had set in motion since her arrival.

Jet clenched her jaw. "He should come with me and get some fresh air and sunshine."

Ben gently removed his hands from Jet's hold and placed

her arms at her side. He gave her a reassuring squeeze. "Each of you has a point. I've done some things that are eating at my insides like cancer. Believe me. I would *love* to be able to wash them away." He turned to Rachael and the downtrodden expression glued itself back on to his face. "Talking about my feelings isn't working either. I'm still here and my head is pounding from trying to unlock the past. But, I do have to make every attempt to get well. Sorry, Jet, I'm staying. Rachael has enough faith for the both of us and that's got to count toward something."

The fear in Ben's eyes was plain to see. Rachael would have given anything to remove the haunted lines from his face.

She couldn't help but wonder what it was that he feared the most. Not knowing the answer to that question was killing her.

Jet must have sensed the same fear lurking in Ben because she flopped back onto the sofa. "Fine. Play Group. But don't come crying to me when you want to have some fun and I'm too busy to care."

Rachael breathed a sigh of relief at having won control. This time at least. One day Jet would get how essential these sessions were to all of them. In the meantime, she had but one purpose. And that was to help Ben unlock his memory.

"Ben, when you write down your thoughts, do you see images as well?"

"No. And don't get mad at me. I can't help my memory loss."

"I know. But." Rachael started tapping her journal till the steady beating became like a timer on a bomb. In three seconds, two seconds, one second, exasperation exploded from somewhere within. "Are you really giving this your best efforts?"

"Are you not listening to me? I write page after page of my deepest, darkest thoughts and I don't hear anybody else reading their journal."

"All right, don't get belligerent. I'll go next." Rachael read:

"I used to believe that everyone had an angel watching over them. At night, they would sit on the ends of beds and watch as mortals slept. That they were the voices inside, telling someone to hurry up or slow down. And that they were the voices telling you to be nice to loved ones even when you were angry with them. Lately I've been wondering if angels are real, because I'm not sure I believe in God anymore. And you can't have one without the other."

She closed her journal. "What do you think about my piece?"

Jet's jaw dropped. "You want to know whether or not I believe in God? That's a pretty snaring question. If I say yes, you'll accuse me of being delusional so my nonexistent problems have to be real. If I say no, I'm in denial so my nonexistent problems must be real. Either way I answer your question, I'm screwed."

Rachael stared at the ceiling and took deep breaths while she pretended to consider this conundrum. She let out a dramatic sigh. "I promise to remain impartial and nonjudgmental. I just want to know if you believe in God, angels, heaven, and the whole afterlife thing. Your answer is really important to me."

Jet eyed her with an air of skepticism. "All right, I'll tell you, but I reserve the right to take it back if you try to bless or exorcise me." She paused. "The whole afterlife thing is a nice concept. Like world peace and a sustainable planet. I wouldn't hold my breath for seeing either of them for real."

Rachael managed a tight smile. Well, she *had* asked for honesty. She turned to Ben. "What did you think of what I wrote?"

"Hell exists because I've been there, done that, and got the T-shirt even if I can't remember buying it. So I guess there has to be a heaven." He reached inside his shirt and took out his necklace, which had a silver cross hanging off its end. "Besides, this belonged to Dad and he was a religious man. It's as much in my blood to believe as it is in Rachael's."

Rachael bit her lower lip until it started to tingle. "I can't believe I'm saying this, but Jet's got a point. I'm not sure I believe in God anymore either."

"I don't believe in ghosts or vampires either." Jet said. "I'm probably the only girl I know who thinks all that stuff is brain rot."

"Probably why you don't have many friends," Rachael mumbled.

"Ghosts are real," whispered Ben. "Very real."

His eyes glazed over as he slipped back into his shell. Rachael decided his imaginary shell was probably the safest place for him at the moment. Because while he was shutting Rachael out, he was shutting Jet out too.

Chapter Six

Jet watched as Ben slipped from nonweird to weird in the time it took for her brow to crease in anger.

Why did he have to keep getting all creepy? Creepy was so much harder to like than hauntingly handsome.

He was staring glassy-eyed at the mirror, and she had a sudden, burning desire to be anywhere but in the living room, which had become too stifling to bear. Besides, Rachael was pushing Group down everyone's throat, and Jet had had enough of being told how to think, feel and act by her father. No way was she going to let a fourteen-year-old brat dictate how her life should be.

She stood up. "I'm going for a swim. Alone."

The latch on the gate was unlocked so she let herself into the pool area. No one else was around, thank Christ. In her haste to get out of the oppressive confines of Group she'd forgotten to grab a towel although she had been dropped off in the middle of the night so she didn't have anything to swim in anyway.

Hoping the pool area continued to remain deserted, she slipped out of her jeans. This wasn't her first time partially skinny-dipping wearing only bra and panties. Her first time had been with Lucas at Narrabeen Lake. Better the lake than the ocean, because the beaches near her house were the type with sheer drops into deep water with strong undercurrents that began only two feet off the shoreline. And if you were brave enough to swim out past the two feet mark, and if you were lucky enough not to get trapped by the current, the waves barreled toward you. Swimming was like fighting off forty-two gallon drums falling from the sky with your legs tied together. Plus there were sharks and she was mortally terrified of surviving an attack that could leave her half eaten alive.

She and Lucas had often swum in the lake on the nights her dad was away on business trips, although she would lie to her mom and tell her she was studying at a friend's house. Passing her exams in school meant her mom had little reason to be suspicious. She reckoned her mom was secretly hitting the booze; she sometimes had a glossed-over expression in her eyes and acted like she was on another planet. Which was great in a way. At least Jet got a short break from the suffocating doctrine her folks labeled parenting.

The first time Jet had forgotten her swimsuit was an accident. The times afterwards were not. And because her father would have spit ballistic missiles if he found out about her nighttime activities, the chance to spite him by getting caught half-naked appealed to her immensely. She didn't need any better motivation than that to go along with Lucas's suggestion.

She smiled at the memory of defying her father. But images of her body and near naked romps with Lucas caused her to shudder till her flesh was alive with goose bumps.

"Guess I'll never be brave enough to go full skinny-dip and now is hardly the time to step out of my comfort zone," she told herself.

She undressed down to her bra and panties and kicked her clothes under a deck chair. The goose bumps made her feel vulnerable, so she used her sneakers as a wedge to lock the gate from the inside. Even if someone was able to get to the gate and see her, they wouldn't be able to get in. Embarrassing? Yes. Dangerous? Possibly no more than anything else she'd done so far.

The pool's tiles sparkled dazzling and white as if they belonged in God's bathroom, beckoning her. When she jumped into the water she squealed with shock as the cold hit her body full force. It might've looked like a giant bathtub, but the water was definitely *not* bath temperature.

She swam a few laps to warm up before she floated toward the edge of the pool, where she leaned her arms over the tiled edging and took in the amazing view of the ocean. The shoreline was a few hundred feet away at the end of a path that wound through swinging palm trees. She imagined the crashing waves and the squawking seagulls were causing quite a ruckus on the beach, but the rooftop was devoid of all noise and activity. Almost like she was the only person alive.

"Maybe tomorrow I'll take a walk down to the beach," she said, secretly wondering if she should stop talking to herself yet knowing the sound of her voice soothed her too much to stop. "If I'm to end up morbid and disturbed like those two, at least let me have a fantastic tan."

Plus, the beach would be noisy. Since arriving, calmness had settled over her, as if she'd spent an entire week meditating. She hoped the quietness inside her head was real, not a curtain concealing bad memories. She didn't want to waste her time mulling over her parents' choice of loony bin. Quite frankly, she was happy to stay in this denial phase forever. Anything was better than accepting the unwelcome consequences.

Repressed memories. Maybe Ben's onto something.

Rachael believed Jet was in denial and Rachael was probably right. Soon enough Jet would be forced to deal with her problems, but at the moment, the natural beauty of the area demanded her attention.

As she breathed in the view, a pang of guilt sent a fresh lashing of goose bumps shimmering across her exposed shoulders. This was a fantastic place and all, but why hadn't her parents come to visit? Even if her father refused to see her, she was surprised by her mom's absence. As mother and daughter they'd shared squabbles and differences of opinions, but the relationship had always been a close one.

Or so she'd thought.

Jet must have once adored her father. Plenty of photos in the family album proved it. Yet there were just as many to disprove it. Anyone flicking through the album could have picked the age when the father/daughter bond was severed.

Around the same time as her puberty blossomed.

The sun forced Jet to close her eyes. Although she was half-naked and vulnerable, she felt freer than ever floating on the water where none of her worries could reach her. Not school. Not final exams. Not even the text messages…

WHORE.

She stopped when her hand hit something in the water. Had she reached the end of the pool already? She opened her eyes to find she was halfway across. She rolled over and paddled in a circle, scanning the bottom of the pool to see if an automatic cleaner was slurping its way around the perimeter. But the water was crystal clear. Nothing on the bottom or on the sides either.

Something brushed up against her leg. "What the—"

She held her breath and put her face under the water, squinting into the depths. She realized that growing panic was stinging her nostrils, not chlorine.

The pool was empty.

What the hell was going on?

Something bumped into her again, almost knocking the wind out her. Her panic soared. She scanned every inch of the pool for her invisible attacker, who had to be a brilliant white in color to blend so perfectly into the background. Yet no matter how hard she scrutinized the water, she saw nothing.

So why was she sure something was swimming past her, purposely bumping into her?

Something grabbed her foot and dragged her to the bottom.

But she was quick to react, maybe because she'd grown up near the water. She held her breath, and all she got was a little water up her nose. But it didn't burn like usual, which she found strange and almost dreamlike.

Of course this is a dream, her mind screamed. She was in a clear body of water and something invisible was attacking her. What other explanation was there?

Except that this was real.

She kicked at her unseen assailant yet her legs touched nothing solid. Despite the temptation to open her mouth to scream, the survivalist part of her brain told her to do so would result in her drowning.

She'd heard drowning was supposed to be calming. Nothing could be further from the truth. Terror gripped her. Her insides scrambled to become her outsides, and her outsides were burrowing down toward her toes.

This is it. I'm going to die for real this time.

As quickly as the assault had begun, the unseen *thing* let go of her foot and she floated to the surface. Gasping for breath, she flailed and kicked toward the edge of the pool.

Before she could reach the edge, she was attacked once

more. This time the wind was knocked out of her as something barreled into her left side and pushed her off course. Had her attacker severed her spinal cord? Was that why she felt no pain? Was someone keeping a science experiment in the pool but had forgotten to tell the guests?

She had the feeling something was defending its territory. And this something was now pushing her toward the edge of the pool as though its intent was to crush her.

Insane thoughts kept her mind busy so at least her mouth stayed shut and didn't fill with water. Until one final, stupid thought exploded into her head:

Oh God, please don't let me die now. My underwear isn't coordinated.

She hauled herself to the edge of the pool and burst out of the water like a performing seal. She rushed to throw on her jeans and top. At the gate she grabbed her shoes and gave a quick glimpse over her shoulder.

There was nothing in the water or clawing its way out of the pool. Nothing at all.

Chapter Seven

Ben came round the corner and bumped into Jet. She let out an ear-splitting scream that sent a flash of an orange sky across his vision. He had to force his eyes to remain open. Her T-shirt clung to her chest. Unable to remove his attention from her erect nipples, he stared as if he was seeing a seminaked girl for the first time. Bad manners aside, he was male and helpless to stop it.

"Hey, you're soaking wet," he said.

Jet, blushing, covered her chest with her arm. "Yeah, I fell in. Clumsy me. I should get changed before I get a cold."

He blocked her path, ignoring the nervous expression that flickered across her face. "Wait. I came to tell say you were right."

"That's great. But I gotta go."

What was wrong with her? He was taken aback by her sudden hostility and sensed she was annoyed at him. After the episode in Group, he'd expected her to be thrilled to see him, but she was trying to sidestep her way around him. But he was used to dodging things that could kill you. Blocking a girl half his size posed no problem at all.

"Didn't you hear me? You were right. I do need to have more fun. Is it too late to take you up on your offer?"

She hugged her arms tightly to her chest, adding to her seductive innocence. For all he knew he smiled, laughed or meowed; his head reeled with her closeness. Lost. Dreaming.

Entranced. He continued to block her path. It seemed like forever since he'd had contact with a beautiful girl, and he was afraid to lose this chance.

"Seeing as you're already wet…"

"What are you doing here, Ben? You said you wanted to stay and play Group with Rachael." Her harsh tone squashed his bravado like she'd taken a sledgehammer to an egg.

Yep. Her hostility was definitely directed at him. Where was the flirty girl, and when was she coming back? He wanted *her*, not this sodden stranger with the viper tongue.

"What you said earlier made sense. Maybe I'll never remember the war so maybe I'll never get well enough to leave. Might as well enjoy myself while I'm here, wouldn't you agree?"

He reached for her and pulled her against him, not caring if he got his clothes wet.

Jet pushed him away. "I would have to disagree. It's too cold. Besides…I…I forgot my bikini."

"Even better."

"No, Ben. Not better. It's a very, very bad idea."

She shoved him hard, finally pushing her way past. He spun, his jaw practically hitting his knees in shock, but she had already disappeared, taking his good mood with her. All that was left was the dark, seething anger that exploded from beneath the surface and overtook his senses.

"You're nothing but a prick tease," he shouted.

He kicked at the gate, reveling in the loud bang that echoed off the wall. His nostrils flared in and out and his teeth were almost ground down to the roots. In a blinding rage he stormed across to the soda machine he'd spied under an awning earlier and started punching its metal sides.

The motion was soothing to the soul, though the metal was proving stronger than flesh and bone. It hung on in there like a dam wall in a flood. His knuckles grew redder and redder as again and again he pounded, showing enough restraint not to break the glass or his hands. Even the little bug in his head was nodding approval at his control. Yet Ben was so close to putting his fist through the glass front despite the burning need to both inflict and accept pain.

Just one good punch and the glass would break and slice his hand open. All that blood…

An image of a bloodied body flashed into his mind. More and more images flashed across his eyes. A dead body… Eyes wide open… Dogs licking at the bloody stump where the head used to be.

"Get the hell out of my head!"

This time he kicked the front of the machine with his boot. A loud noise cracked the air, followed by a sliver in the glass that threatened to shower splintery shards everywhere, but the machine held firm. He fought to control the tornado of rage by rummaging around inside his pocket till he gripped a few loose coins. Using brute force he shoved the coins into the slot.

And waited. And waited some more.

His blood boiled when nothing came out and he almost tossed his head back to laugh with maniacal glee. Stupid machine had just given him another reason to kick it. Why not? No one else was close enough to take the brunt of his rage.

He lifted his foot and curled his hand into a fist—

The image of a small girl jumped into his vision. Dirty face, knotted hair, frightened eyes, hands held out in front of her. She seemed to be pleading to him to stop.

"Why should I stop? Please tell me."

He hadn't really expected an answer; he closed his eyes to let her terror enter him so he could remember what had frightened her. But the girl in his visions disappeared and his inner turmoil followed.

His anger evaporated slowly, draining out of him like thick sludge.

He stood in front of the vending machine feeling as if his insides were hollowed out. And he wished for the anger to return, because he had no energy left to brace for the oncoming emptiness that was always unbearable.

A vision of his mother sprang to mind. She'd always hated it when his anger got him into fights. Sometimes she'd hit Ben with a strap and ask him how he liked it.

"I need you, Mom," he said, his voice barely above a whisper. "Where are you? Why aren't you here?"

Ben thumped the machine once more, though all the force had left his punch. "Come on, come on."

He banged the machine with his forehead repeatedly as the rage drained from him, thick and slow, taking its time as though savoring the sensation.

"Don't give up without a fight. Please. Hit me back. Come on."

Why was his anger so fleeting? He was desperate to hold onto his rage, for its aftereffect came stalking like bad food, ten times worse coming out than going in. It would be upon him soon. And despite anticipating its arrival, he was still taken unawares.

He was never prepared for the dreadful emptiness. It doused everything he was, like a flame plunged into cold water. Nothingness invaded his body. It terrified him, this nothingness that shut down everything till he was only a tiny speck of light in the middle of a computer screen.

He always felt numb. Dead.

And then as if the power was abruptly restored, he began to feel again. Little flickers of sensation that could only be described as sadness, rushing him, engulfing him with great shame till he was crying. He buried his face in his hands.

Then guilt rocked him. Like a bolt of acid, it coursed toward him with such speed and purpose that when he took its full brunt he screamed out loud. Finally, a cloud of sorrow, dark and thick, poured down and drenched him, pretending to cleanse him with kindness. But this shrouding mist was an entity too dark to know goodness.

Like a haunted merry-go-round, morbid sensations swirled around and around. He fell to the ground, writhing and screaming in agony.

Is this how life is for me now?

The little bug in the back of his mind said, "Hasn't it *always* been this way?"

He hated answering the little bug. Hated talking to him but would else could he do? Cut off his head? If he were guaranteed that the drastic measure would stop the torment he'd have cut off every limb.

Lying on the ground, Ben wished he could seep into the cement. His insides felt raw, as though scooped out and put in a blender. Worse was the realization that he was unable to hold onto any true emotion for any length of time, as if his hatred was just a mask.

For the first time, he'd told Rachael the truth. Group sessions were no longer working. Maybe they'd never worked. Nor would they.

I am beyond salvation.

Years of reading his daddy's Bible was enough for him to have learned the rules. He'd committed sins. Just because he couldn't remember them, didn't mean they were any less real.

At last his senses resumed normal activity and his knees buckled with shame that he'd forced himself onto Jet.

"What the hell was I thinking?" he said aloud.

Give yourself a break, he thought. You knew exactly what was running through your brain.

She had smelled alive, and he'd allowed himself to get caught up in the intoxicating memories of summers on the lake. Jumping into the water off the gorge, surfing the rapids on makeshift kayaks, catching a yard-long bass and trying to get the thing home on a bicycle, the thrill of cheering on a bucking bull at the rodeo.

Yet, *had* he pushed himself on her?

Now the numbness had disappeared, he could see in his mind how he'd backed away from her but something had shoved him from behind.

Slowly, he hauled his weakened body up off the floor. His stomach lurched and he wanted to throw up, but he bit back what had to be bile because he couldn't quite recall his last meal. Was it days or weeks? It didn't matter. His only concern was finding Jet to apologize.

As he stood up he saw something in the corner of his eye. It looked like a shadow, except—

He saw it again. A shadow, only white and racing across the wall.

It disappeared around a corner. Ben searched for what the shadow might belong to, but he was alone. It had to be a trick of the light.

To his left now, another trick of light jumped into the air. Following its trail closely, it twirled up like a mini tornado where it morphed into a cloud, which was impossible, yet strangely normal at the same time. After all, he saw and heard weird shit all the time. Why not shadow ghosts?

His eyes had to be deceiving him.

The shadows fell out of the clouds and came spiraling toward the ground. Fast. Like a whirlpool, spinning and spinning straight for him.

Ben supposed he was hallucinating. Sometimes migraines gave him white spots in his vision. They were called auras. Sometimes these auras came without the escort of a headache. When they did they were called silent migraines. He reckoned he was in the middle of a silent migraine attack. What other explanation was there for his blurred vision? Shadows weren't white. And they did not shape shift.

Even as he told himself he had finally slipped into crazy land with no return ticket, a shadow crossed the wall in the direction Jet had just taken.

The shadow stopped and this time Ben could have sworn the shadow gestured at him to stay put.

He had no intention of obeying a hallucination. He took off after it, knocking over chairs and tables as he hurtled to catch the retreating white shape. He told himself to hold onto his sanity.

I am not crazy. I've seen these shadows before.

These shadows were the same as the milky-white images he saw every day in the mirror in the living room.

Chapter Eight

Jet managed to put the scare in the pool out on her mind though remnants hung on like cobwebs. But standing outside a door with the word ART ROOM painted on it, another chill ran up her spine as the horror of the attack came flooding back to her.

With a shake of her head, she told herself not to be stupid. She could have kicked herself for letting her imagination run wild. She had never believed in ghosts. A loony bin was the last place she wanted to pick up the bad habit of a morbid worship-cum-fascination with the undead.

She suspected the sudden chill was a result of Ben saying ghosts were real and her overstimulated teenage brain was eager to believe *anything* a cute guy told her. That was the only reason she was receptive to the idea.

Good one, Jet. Way to show everyone you're not crazy.

If only Ben had not shouted out she that was a tease. That had stung. Yet what hurt and disappointed her more was the use of name calling as his best defense. Was he blind not to have noticed how scared to death she'd been? Was he such an idiot he couldn't tell the difference between shivering with cold and shaking with fear? Staring at her nipples was not the type of comfort she'd wanted.

"What is wrong with men? If you give them the vaguest notion you're contemplating sex with them you're a slut. If you refuse, you're a tease. And why is it that the girl gets stuck with the bad reputation?"

Talking to herself felt good. Venting felt good.

"Ben can go to hell. All men can. I hate them all."

She jerked the art room door open and the heated stare of a dozen set of eyes latched onto her. She stopped.

"Hello?" she called out and was surprised when her voice fell flat. She guessed this large room with its high ceiling would have given off an echo.

Where were the artists? The room was bright and she suspected they were hidden behind their easels, busily scratching their brushes back and forth across the canvases. At least the scratching noise was her explanation for the unusual sound that snaked around the room as if a current of live electricity was on the loose.

An empty canvas stood in the center of the room. Someone spoke from inside the ring of canvases. "Join us."

"Oh, I'm not the creative type. But thanks anyway."

Eyes seemed to follow her every movement as she crept along the wall where their artwork was hung. Weird. Where the living room was bright and cheery, the art room was bright yet unwelcoming. Icy cold, too, colder than the pool. She wrapped her arms around her waist to ward off the advancing chill and took her first look at a painting.

A single, soulless eye gazed out at her from behind a thick smearing of dark paint. The horrible image reminded her of B-grade horror movie posters, or maybe she was just creeped out from what Ben had revealed in his journal. The dark, depressing discourse on his fighting in a war he didn't believe in seemed to have hit a nerve.

"I suppose I'm not surprised he has such dark thoughts. Why else is he here?"

She let out a heavy sigh. Wanting Ben to be normal, and hating to admit that he wasn't, upset her more than she liked, and for a good reason. Ben was filled with unhappiness, which made him no different to half the people on the planet, but half the people on the planet weren't in a ghost-town healing center trying to unclog their trapped despair. Which meant that if Ben was unfixable, what hope had she of getting well?

Staring at the painting was getting her even more creeped out, if that were possible. She had to leave.

She'd almost made it to the door when a pale girl rushed her, pinning her up against the wall.

"You don't belong here. Get out." The girl spun and sped off to the other side of the room. A plume of white haze followed obediently behind.

The bright lights are making her appear ghostly. That's all.

Jet started to choke on paint fumes, coughing till her throat burned. As she took a step toward the door, she tripped. He foot buckled underneath her and she went to the floor. As she fell, a memory rushed up to meet her.

* * *

"Why do you put up with him?" Jet asked her mother. The afternoon sun seemed to have slipped behind the sofa while they were in the living room taking folded clothes from one laundry hamper and dividing them into three others. Feeling brave, she added, "Tell him you want your car fixed or you want a new dress. Ask him to take you on a romantic weekend."

Her mother narrowed her eyes yet Jet saw a glint of real

fear in them. "Mind your own business."

A few folded garments later Jet glanced at her mother and was overcome with a feeling of protectiveness. "You could divorce him. You know you'd get fifty percent of his assets."

Her mother gasped. "Julliet Rose. Who is putting these ideas into your head?"

Too late. Jet had taken it too far. Yet she was only repeating what Lucas had said.

Her mother began racing around the house, opening every cupboard door and banging it closed again, as though enjoying the sound of the slamming doors. Jet followed her from room to room, but her mother was an uncatchable streak of pale pink. When Jet found her mom in the laundry room, her head was inside the washer.

"Are you checking for bugs?" Jet asked.

The way her mother was carrying on should have made Jet laugh, but instead it stopped her heart. Her dad was the type to bug the house simply to hear how his women plotted ways to find his hidden money.

Her mother slammed down the lid of the washer. "Who is putting these ideas into your head?"

"No one," she squeaked.

Her mother dug her bony hand into her arm. Long fingernails pressed deep enough to hit marrow. Her mother wasn't going to back down till Jet blabbed about everything.

Relief washed over Jet since she was dying to tell someone about Lucas.

She grinned. "Oh, all right. But you're gonna freak. So please stay cool. His name is Lucas and he's my boyfriend."

"A kid from school?"

"Not exactly."

She was inches away from her mother's face, so close Jet

could smell her breath. Was that alcohol she detected? Couldn't be. Her mom never drank anything stronger than apple cider.

"What do you mean not exactly?"

So Jet told her mother all about Lucas. She gushed and blushed and went on and on about how wonderful he was.

"How long have you two been dating?"

"About a week."

Her mother was not smiling. Why was she not smiling? Jet was in love, and her mother was acting like such a bitch about it.

"You're lying," said her mom.

"All right. He's not a boy. He's twenty-three and we've been dating for two months."

"You have to break it off with him. Today, before your father flies in from Jakarta. You know the rules. No boyfriends till school is finished."

Jet glared at her mother. "Till I leave this house, you mean. And by the way, that's Dad's rule, not mine. I'm not a kid anymore. I'm almost eighteen."

"You turned seventeen a few months ago. Think about your exams, love. You can break it off till your exams are over." Her mother began shaking her. As though realizing what she was doing she loosened her grip. But only slightly. Jet was still unable to pull her arm out.

Jet wriggled until her arm finally came free. "How out of touch with reality are you? He won't wait a few months."

"He will if he loves you."

"You know nothing about love." Jet ran out of the room with tears stinging her eyes.

Moments later, her mother entered Jet's bedroom and sat on the end of the bed. "You're right. What do I know about love? Your father and I drifted apart years ago. I have no idea how to win him back."

"Tape fifty bucks to your body."

Jet regretted saying it the moment the words had flown out of her mouth. Why was she saying cruel things to her mother? The fact they were both trapped in a horrible home with no escape should've made them friends, not enemies.

She was gripped by fear that if her mother never smiled again it would be because of her, and she'd spent eternity in hell for her part in the miserable home life they shared. If the photos in the family album, the ones prior to puberty stripping the smiles off their faces the way a Band-Aid would, were any indication, once theirs had been a happy home.

But a family can only hold onto its secrets for so long before the secrets grow teeth and come seeking blood.

"I'm sure you know more about love than me," Jet told her mom. "I can tell Lucas is already bored with bringing me home by six each night. What we have will die on its own. Can't I enjoy it while it lasts?" She reached for her mother's hand. "We can keep this between us."

Secrecy must have appealed to her mother because she rewarded Jet with a smile. Weak, and Jet suspected forced, but this smile was more than she'd seen from her mother in a very long time. Jet also suspected her mother's smirk had more to do with keeping something from her husband than sharing a treasured moment with her daughter. But what else could Jet do but accept the truce? She had to keep Lucas a secret.

* * *

Jet woke up. Her head and her ankle were throbbing. Groaning, she dragged herself up off the floor and her hand pressed down onto a paintbrush. Handy thing to leave lying around where someone could trip on it, she thought. But had someone left it there accidentally or intentionally?

Her ankle wasn't broken, just badly twisted. So she sat on the floor rubbing it gently. Then she tended to her forehead. No sign of bleeding. Also no sign of the girl who'd rammed her against the wall, though Jet was sure she was slinking around somewhere. And probably laughing her chemically whitened head off.

"Has anyone told her vampires are so last year?" Jet groaned.

She sniffed back tears, wanting her mom more than ever. She badly needed a hug and would have latched onto a grizzly for comfort. But she was alone, and she had to concede that whether by choice or by force, her mom was not coming to see her.

When at last her ankle was strong enough to hold her weight, she limped back to her room, telling herself that when she saw her dad next she'd give him a piece of her mind for leaving her to rot in this loony bin.

But she wouldn't. It took more guts than she possessed.

Chapter Nine

Rachael could tell from Jet's swollen, red eyes she'd been crying. Based on her limp, she'd injured her foot.

"Are you okay?" Rachael asked. She heard an undercurrent of suspicion in her tone instead of concern and couldn't understand she didn't trust the other girl at all, because it was so unlike her to not like anyone.

Jet winced when her foot knocked against the coffee table. "Why are men such jerks?"

Evidence suggested Jet and Ben had fought, but Rachael refused to believe Ben would harm anyone, most of all a girl.

Rachael let her eyes travel up and down Jet, learning nothing. "Probably a good thing you feel that way. We're not supposed to fraternize in here. Not what you'd call helpful in the healing process."

Jet reached for the tissues stored under the coffee table, grabbed one, and blew her nose. "Shut up about the healing process. Nothing is wrong with me. Besides, why would I want to go home?"

Rachael leaned over to offer comfort but jerked away as though shocked by a bolt of electricity. Physical contact was her Achilles heel; it would take her apart. So she clutched at the sofa cushions instead.

Who knew inanimate objects could bring comfort?

At last the warmth of empathy began to flood through her. She was concerned for Jet, and not a moment too soon.

She had started to worry that her sense of compassion had left her for good.

"Is your home life really awful?" Rachael asked, hugging the cushion closer to her chest.

Jet nodded and wiped a strand of hair out of her eyes. "My father treats my mom and me like slaves. He's super rich but we always have to take our own food and drink if we go anywhere. Which we hardly ever do because the price of fuel keeps going up and up." Her left hand moved up through the air in a motion of a fish swimming for the surface. "Mom has been selling her old stuff on the internet so she can buy new stuff. I mean, I'm into the whole recycling thing but that's pushing it too far."

"Maybe he's saving up to buy something special."

Jet's eyes shifted. "Whatever he's saving up for it's worth over a million dollars. He showed us the bank statement one night after he'd had one wine too many. And you know what made the whole situation worse? We were eating sausages—which I hate—and mashed potatoes—which I sort of like, but after eating potato something-or-other for seven nights straight, you end up wishing to never see another potato again."

A fresh bout of tears sprang from Jet's eyes and she used the tissue to dab them. "He never takes us out to dinner, not even for special occasions. The kids in school are always talking about how they went to Mexican or Italian restaurants for their birthday. We went out to dinner once."

Her face twisted into a grimace. "And not even to a fancy place either. Just a stupid buffet where kids under twelve ate for free. Tells you how long ago our special family outing was. *And* we left without eating dessert."

She closed her eyes. Tiny tears rolled down her cheek. Rachael felt bad for watching them, yet at the same time she wondered if perhaps Jet was exaggerating. No one could hate their father that badly.

"God, I wish he was dead," Jet whispered with such vehemence she might as well have shouted.

Rachael gasped. "What an awful thing to wish for. You should never say that, not even as a joke. God *does* grant people their wishes, you know. Maybe not wishes like winning the lottery or the ability to fly, but He grants wishes like sunshine on a wedding day or good marks in an exam. What if your wish came true?"

Jet gave her an incredulous stare. "I just told you I wish it did. I hate him. Hate him! Hate him!" She began shouting at the top of her voice. "I wish he was dead. I wish he was dead."

Rachael was almost frothing at the mouth in hysteria. To wish someone dead was not taken lightly. There would be repercussions. She dug her nail into the cushion till she was sure the soft lining would spill out. "Never say that. He's your father."

Jet shrugged her shoulders and looked away. Her anger had apparently dissipated, and Rachael was taken aback at how quickly that had occurred.

"Maybe. Maybe not," Jet said. "Mom got pregnant with me practically on their first date. She told him I was his but he later found out she was seeing another guy at the same time. So maybe I am someone else's bastard child."

If that were true, Rachael supposed that could explain the way he treated his wife and child. And that explained why Jet was driven by a need to be loved by the man she called her father. And why she had acted out by taking an overdose in order to get his attention.

If that were true.

"How do you know this?" asked Rachael. "Did you

mother tell you?"

"No. My cousin, Steve. I was such a mess always wondering why my father hated me so much that one morning I decided to run away. I skipped school and spent the day at the beach. My cousin is a lifeguard and he let me hang around the clubhouse. Eventually I told him why I was running away. That's when he told me about my parents." Jet paused. "Man, was I upset. The fact that I could be another person's child took a bit of getting used to. But knowing the truth about the man I called my father, well…afterwards everything made sense."

Rachael frowned. Cousin Steve was hardly the most credible source of the truth. "Maybe your cousin made it up."

A dark scowl crossed over Jet's face. "Girls spread lies. Boys spread the truth. Believe me, lies are much easier to deal with." She gazed at Rachael, eyes twinkling bright with tears and held out her arms in an open embrace. "Hey, I could use a hug right now."

Rachael must have had a horrified look on her face and Jet must have seen it. By the time Rachael could remove it, the damage was done.

Jet's face turned bright red and scrunched like a dried chili. "Aw, come on. That's hardly fair. I pour out my soul to you and you act like I want to feel you up. What the hell is wrong with you?"

Rachael bowed her head. Shame picked at her skin, making it itch and burn. No matter how much she wanted to empathize with the other girl, physical contact was not an option. It meant establishing a relationship, and she could not allow herself to have that bond.

Jet ended the silence by blowing her nose. "Fine. Be a basket case. So what about your parents? What are they like?"

"I wouldn't know. I don't have any."

She watched as Jet's expression flicked from surprised to sympathetic to curious in rapid succession.

"Oh? Oh! Who do you live with?"

"Lots of people."

"Did your parents die? Well, obviously they died. Oh, wait, maybe they gave you up for adoption. Jeez, I'm sorry. Maybe I should just shut up now."

Rachael giggled as Jet squirmed, clearly discomfited by the way the conversation was going. Was she wrong about Jet? Was Jet simply an ordinary teenager who yearned for her father's love as other ordinary teenagers did? Or was something else responsible for bringing about this sudden change of heart? Try this on for size, Rachael thought. Am I beginning to like Jet simply because she no longer likes Ben? This seemed the more credible explanation and she cringed inwardly for thinking it.

She noticed that Jet was still waiting for her to say something. So she told her the truth. "I have a father. At least I want to believe I do, but a part of me says I'm going to get hurt if I don't face reality." She paused. "I feel like I've lived my life through someone else and when they wake up I'll discover I never existed."

Rachael was gripped by a compulsive need to tell Jet the one thing she was dreading admitting to herself and the words flew out of her mouth before she could stop them. "I think I'm losing hope."

"No no no." Jet jumped up. "Don't lose hope. Jeez, does this have anything to do with what I said before about not believing in God? Forget about that. You have a right to believe in whatever you want to. Gosh, last season I truly believed fake tans were out and I spent all summer as white as a ghost."

Rachael laughed so loud she snorted. Once started, she couldn't stop laughing, and after a while her cheeks and stomach hurt but it felt good to have a moment of hysterics. Even though she adored Ben, he was a poor provider of comic inspiration.

Both girls were laughing when Ben came into the room moments later. Rachael caught the way Jet shot him a fierce look before quickly averting her gaze. He looked away, too, as if they were co-conspirators. Rachael stopped laughing. Jealousy flooded through her till her skin burned with nausea.

How dare they keep secrets from her.

She experienced another rare emotion—wrath. Her blood boiled and her fists clenched till her fingernails dug into the palms of her hands.

What a fool to believe Jet was making an effort to befriend her, when all along she'd been using Rachael as a way of avoiding Ben.

Rachael was glad now she'd refused to give Jet that hug.

* * *

Later that afternoon Rachael had her head buried in her journal, reading over what she'd written yesterday though it seemed like ages ago.

The sound of a heavy sigh made her look up.

Jet sat staring out the window, her eyes busily scanning the outside world. "I wonder where they are. I honestly thought they would have visited me by now."

Rachael took a wild guess that Jet was talking about her parents. She closed her journal, hating to admit that she had written nothing at all today. Finding it difficult to get into the mood, she blamed the apathy that Ben and Jet had for these sessions for trickling down onto her. Apathy was another new emotion for her, and one she didn't like.

"There are strict rules about visitors here," she explained. "Your parents can't just come and go as they please. Same goes for cell phones, laptops, and any other typical source of communication. Notice the lack of pigeons? Anyway, outside influences impede our healing."

Jet spun in her chair. Her face was aflame with hostility. "Have you heard a word I've said? Let me spell it out for you. There. Is Nothing. Wrong. With. Me. God, you are such a pest."

Rachael wondered if the reason she wasn't retaliating was due to apathy. Jet got up and left the room but in less than a minute she was back and brandishing a teddy bear, which she waved in Rachael's face.

"Did you do this?" Jet shoved the stuffed toy close enough that Rachael could read the NOT SUITABLE FOR BABIES label. She then stormed over to where Ben was sitting on the sofa and shoved the teddy bear under his nose. "Did you? Huh. Which one of you is playing tricks on me?"

"What are you going on about?" Ben swatted at the stuffed toy.

Jet jerked it away. "Which one of you read through my journal? This is *my* teddy bear. You'd only know this was *my* bear if you'd read *my* journal."

Rachael gaped at her, aghast at the suggestion. "I never touched your journal. That would be a breach of confidentiality."

"Who else could have brought it here? Huh? Tell me —"

Jet stopped midsentence and Rachael watched in fascination as the red tinge on her cheeks turned into a bright purple hue. Her lips moved but made no sound. If she went into cardiac arrest now, more than CPR would be needed to revive her.

At last Jet spoke and her voice croaked in agony. "I can't believe my parents dropped this off and left without saying a word."

She ran from the room and Rachael was surprised to discover she had neither the will nor the energy to go after her. This feeling went beyond apathy, she realized. More like chronic fatigue, and fatigue in the battle to win over the negative vortex was not the outcome she wanted. She also recognized that if she was to change her current mind set, she'd need inspiration. And inspiration meant venturing outside the living room.

Could she handle leaving her safety zone? Outside was a bad world that terrified her. But she had to. She couldn't find inspiration within. So she got up and followed the direction Jet had just taken, but continued passed their shared bedroom.

As Rachael crept along the hallway, with her hand running along the wall like she was blind and reading a hidden set of directions in the brickwork, she told herself that she was venturing into this bad world for the sake of her beloved Ben. He needed her to remain a well of positivity. Although she'd soon drown him in her figurative well of positivity if he didn't start getting better.

Why was he not getting better? The plan was supposed to be a simple one. Heal the wounds and be freed. But he was not getting any better. If anything, he was getting worse.

A jolt of shivers ran spiderlike along her fingers. Her hand kicked back, as if a sharp pin had stabbed her. Her mind was screaming at her go back. Go anywhere. *Run! Turn around and run! Run as fast you can!*

The words ART ROOM were scratched into the wooden door. If she was going to tackle Jet's and Ben's combined negativity, she would need to recharge on everything that was its opposite. And art had long been considered one of the most powerful means of positive stimulation.

Despite her hand itching and her mind screaming at her to run away, this had to be the right place. She pushed open the door, breathing deeply, preparing her mind for the flow of artistic stimuli, yet barely had she taken a step inside the room when the luminous white walls appeared to rush toward her. Her lungs filled with a thick, sleep-inducing fog.

Wracked by a coughing fit, she pushed on farther into the room. She was wrong to think inspiration could be found in this room. Oppression ruled here.

"I'm here for Ben," she reminded herself, "and I'm not leaving until I get what I came for."

Her heart sank when she saw that the walls were plastered with painted canvases that were dark enough to make her want to jump off a cliff. Still, she forced herself to walk around the room. Artwork adorned every inch of every wall. Even the floor was overflowing with canvases.

Behind the easels, dozens and dozens of artists painted, possibly a hundred of them. Rachael ceased breathing momentarily to avoid detection. A team of monkeys could tell that everyone in this room was beyond help. If Ben didn't make a real good attempt at unblocking his wartime memories, he could end up here.

"How are these supposed to inspire me?" she asked as she stood in front of a painting of a dead and bloated…whatever it was.

"It's a self-portrait," a voice said from behind.

Rachael spun. A few feet away stood a girl. She had a sickly, gray complexion, but her hair was vivid white and she had the palest blue eyes Rachael had ever seen. Quite possibly the girl had sat in a vat of bleach for years.

The girl smiled. Nothing warm or inviting in that smile. Menacing, Rachael thought, which put her on guard.

"I'm tired of painting myself. But it's all I do. Look." The girl rummaged through the canvases on the floor. She withdrew one that had an indigo blue background and a single pale, bloodshot eye staring from the center. Pointing to the middle of the room where a crystal bowl containing a colorful array of fruit sat on a table, she continued. "This is supposed to be that."

She tore off and went in search of another painting, which she found, and with a sort of timid pride, she shoved the canvas at Rachael. Similar to the first canvas, except with a dark red background, and equally appalling. The girl cast that canvas aside and produced another painting, and another and another. Rachael was quick to notice the pattern, and she began to back away. All the paintings were of the same image—a single, bloodshot eye that looked as if it belonged to someone who was being buried alive.

"No matter what I paint, whether it is clouds, fruit, sunsets, every picture turns out the same. They are all pictures of me passing judgment on myself."

When Rachael moved, she felt the eyes in the pictures following her. "You have captured it rather well. Maybe you should come to my Group sessions."

Even as the words left her mouth, she regretted them. The girl's pale eyes lit up, yet before Rachael could take back what she'd said, a guy appeared—her twin maybe, for he was just as deathly pale. When he scowled, icy arrows laced with contempt shot outwards and hit Rachael square in the face. He dragged the girl back to her easel, and Rachael was secretly glad to have her forcibly removed.

"I was once like you," the girl called out as Rachael hurried toward the door. "You'll be in here soon. There is no escaping your fate. You belong here with us."

Chapter Ten

Ben knew the girls' quarters were out of bounds, but he had to speak to Jet and waiting till she came out of hiding would be too late. Their bedroom door was ajar. Craning his head at an angle, he saw Jet was lying on her bed facing the wall. It appeared as though she was asleep although something told him she was wide awake.

He tapped on the door, and it moved inward another few inches. The walls were pale green in color, the carpet speckled grey. Two canvas prints featuring rainforests watched over twin wrought-iron beds. The room was long but narrow, so the two small bed heads sat butted up against each other with only one small table between the two. An assortment of coffee mugs, photo frames, candles, jewelry, pens, and hair clips cluttered the side tables.

On the wall directly facing Ben was a small window with the blinds open halfway. Frosted glass prevented anything from the outside shining in so the room was dim, despite it being the middle of the day.

Jet was still as a corpse, face down sprawled atop the bedcovers, which featured a bright blue and yellow swirling pattern, like those in the hotel rooms where his mom had worked.

"What do you want?" Jet groaned.

He struggled to hear her voice, muffled by the pillow. The little bug in his head held up a sign that read SHE

HATES YOU! Served him right if she did. But if she hated him because of his actions he'd never be able to look himself in the mirror again. He had to fix this. He had strong feelings for her, and because of the way she'd flirted with him earlier, he was sure she had similar feelings for him. He needed to know if she still had them.

He had no one else to blame for screwing things up with Jet. And why had he called her a prick tease? Even a moron could tell you the fastest way to end a relationship was to call a chick a derogatory name.

It's because you hate yourself, and you'll never be satisfied until everyone else hates you too, crowed the little bug in his head.

He shook off the thought. Probably true, but he wanted to change. He wanted things to go back to the way they were when Jet had first arrived. The happiest two days of his life were with Jet, where, for a brief moment his mind had been clear of the fog and he'd felt normal.

"I wanted to say sorry for calling you a tease. I was out of line. Couldn't even tell you why I said it."

Nowhere in his mind did he picture her jumping off the bed and running toward him with open arms, but neither had he pictured stone cold silence. Something in the middle was what he'd hoped for. Her icy snub was like a punch in the stomach.

She had her back facing him but he detected a slight movement. He waited. Still nothing. He must have imagined the movement just like he imagined everything else.

He was ready to give up and leave when she spoke.

"I guess this place is enough to get us all a bit crazy."

He let out his breath. At least she was talking to him. For now that was enough to stop to the cogs in his head churning dark thought after dark thought till he was on the verge of puking. Even standing ten feet away from her had a calming effect on his mind; his inner sanctum was more pleasant and much less bloodied.

Would she agree to him following her? Sure, others might see it as stalking but that would be incorrect. She contained the power to soothe a troubled mind. If he could bottle her essence he'd sell millions of this potion to other soldiers who were losing, or had already lost, their minds.

With a start he realized that it wouldn't matter if she let him shadow her or not. As a soldier, and a hunter before that, he was trained to follow things without his prey noticing. He knew a lot of other things, too.

Like how to tell if a tin of household paint was a homemade bomb.

And at what height you could stack dead bodies so they stayed put without toppling over.

And how the instant meals the army gave you to eat were only appetizing to starving dogs and children.

And like how, when nothing else could lift your spirits, Tabasco sauce was awesome at giving a hit.

Why could he remember these details about the war, and not the things that kept his mind locked up?

"You still there?" Jet asked.

"Sorry. I zoned out. I'll leave you alone now."

She rolled over. "No. Don't go."

Her eyes were puffy and red from crying. He flinched. Blood on his hands was easier to wash away than the guilt he felt over making her cry.

"Are you all right?" he asked.

She let out a heavy sigh. "I don't know. I get the feeling I'm in this place because I'm crazy. Is that it? Have I lost my mind?"

He shrugged his shoulders. "The last person you wanna

ask is me. The only reason I know my own name is because it's written on the inside collar of my shirt."

He was relieved to hear she wasn't laughing, because he wasn't joking.

Jet crunched up her brow as though her mind was taking off somewhere else. After a moment she looked up at the ceiling. "I took an overdose of vodka and sleeping pills. And I woke up here. I believed this place was a detox center. Now I wonder if it's something else."

"You mean a nut house? I wonder it all the time. Sometimes I wonder if I tried to kill myself, but every time I wrack my brain to remember, I black out."

Jet sat upright and her eyes hungrily searched his. "Exactly. Something is wrong with this place. Do you sense the weirdness?"

Did he think this place was odder than a one-armed man taking piano lessons? Even now he was struggling to block out the images in the mirror that were beckoning to him. And he was fighting to block out the images of the strange white shadows that had chased after Jet. Some of the shadows had raced across the wall and some of them had jumped into the sky to become clouds.

The little bug interrupted his musings by telling him that his mom would be home soon as it held up a sign that read FIX THE SINK.

Hell yeah, there was something odd about this place.

"You might be onto something," he whispered.

Jet was staring at him with raised eyebrows, as though seeking answers to an unasked question, but he was hard-pressed to elaborate. How could he tell her that he saw things? Admitting he believed in ghosts was one thing, describing them as gymnasts would prove to her that he was nuts. Still, what if they weren't ghosts?

What if his brain was unraveling like a spool of wire, and the white shadows were a forewarning of an aneurism? He got spots in his vision when he got migraines, and he wanted to accept that he lived in a world where anything was possible. Why not see shadows before a seizure?

Jet was talking and he had to concentrate to listen because he was sure he'd missed a part of the conversation.

"It's like we're being drugged or something," she said. "I'm never hungry but I don't remember eating. I smell clean even though I don't remember taking a shower. And look, this empty coffee cup has sat on my bedside table but I swear I haven't boiled the kettle, and why would I when I hate coffee?" Her eyes narrowed. "Plus, I have loads of clothes in the wardrobe, but I wake up every day wearing the same outfit, which is *so* not me."

"I wake up on the sofa without going to sleep," Ben told her. "But forgetfulness is normal for me.'

"Is it, Ben? Is it normal or are we in a mental hospital. Maybe we're some place worse, you, know, like part of a scientific experiment. How else do you explain—"

She stopped. A flicker of dread crossed her eyes and drained her face of all color. Ben could have sworn she was about to say, "How else do you explain the things I've seen?"

"I'm starting to lose perspective on time," she continued. "It feels like I got here a few hours ago, but it also feels like months."

"This place has the same effect on me."

"Am I going to get better?"

A rare smile tugged at his lips. "I thought there was nothing wrong with you."

At least he could still make her laugh. She waved a finger at him "Don't you dare tell Rachael that I said this. She'll never leave me alone. Honestly, I don't know how you can stand it. She's such a bossy boots."

"She's just watching out for me. I'm lucky she cares as much as she does."

He smiled as he realized just how fortunate he was to have someone constantly watching over him, because he was hardly able to do it himself anymore. Plus, she seemed to find some redeemable qualities in him. Left up to him, he'd probably stay broken.

The little bug in his head jumped up with excitement and held up a sign that read, BROKEN. Grinning, it flashed up a memory of his mother putting the cutlery and plates into the dishwasher. She'd told him it was broken, which had made him mad because their house didn't have a dishwasher. The only place his mom had used that modern appliance was at the motel. When Ben took the call from the manager and was told how much the repair bill was, he'd yelled at his mom. In his rage he'd said some nasty things, one of which was that she ought to be locked up. Not just for her safety, but for the entire town's.

His mother's decline into dementia had been slow and stealthy. Nobody had seen it coming. A forgotten moment here and there was nothing out of the ordinary. His mom would blame a head cold for making her forget to take the trash out. When that excuse got old she turned to blaming food additives as the cause of her clouded mind because she had seen reports on TV, although to his knowledge she was eating the same things as usual. When the doctors finally figured out what was wrong with her nothing could be done. No miracle cures. Not even any run-of-the-mill conventional cures. Only care.

Maybe the curse of forgetfulness was payback for telling his mom she should be locked up. Or maybe it was something worse. What if his memory was not merely repressed, but what if he was suffering from hereditary dementia, only he'd somehow developed an adolescent version?

Jet gave a nervous laugh. "Jesus, Ben, you're going to break the door. Loosen up, will you?"

He didn't know he was gripping the door handle so tightly. He let go but he would never loosen up. Army life had conditioned that luxury out of him. Complacency got soldiers killed. Good soldiers had nerves as sharp as razor blades. Good warriors danced on the edge of the future to anticipate the moves of their enemy.

But Jet was not his enemy. He was.

"I just wanted to make sure we were okay. Goodnight, Jet."

* * *

A little while later, Ben was wedged under the sink. Water was dripping from the pipe and onto his face. He'd just finished sticking the S-bend section of the sink back onto the main pipe when someone tapped him on the knee.

"What are you doing?" Jet asked.

"The sink has to be fixed before she gets home."

"Before who gets home? Your mom? She's not here. None of our parents are. Ben, are you sure you're all right?"

He opened his mouth to answer. He closed it again.

No, I'm not all right. I have no idea where I am or what I'm doing.

For a second he was at home in Riggins, but he realized

he couldn't be there because he was here. But where was here?

The bright light was stinging his eyes. He didn't want to accept that he was crying. But his face was wet with tears that he'd held in for so long. Male pride told him good things came to men who stuck their head under the sink so nobody could witness their moments of weakness. If only time would speed up so he could slip into the eternal dementia he feared yet welcomed at the same time. Anything was better than constantly shifting in and out of realities.

Even death.

Chapter Eleven

Rachael woke with goodness bubbling inside her chest. Today their group session was going to be great. Ben was going to be pulled out of the deep rut of depression and be on his way to making a full recovery. No, make that better than full recovery, if that were at all possible.

She struggled to find words that topped splendid, magnificent, and tremendous but found there were none. Instead she told herself that Ben was going to make a splendid, magnificent, and tremendous recovery. What did it matter that she'd told herself this every morning since arriving? What mattered was this morning every living fiber of her body believed it.

Would she then start working on fixing Jet? She did love new assignments.

As Rachael walked along the corridor she realized just how much she missed school. The spirit of education always warmed her, as if education was a vivacious aunt from abroad who showered you with the smell of Africa whenever she embraced you.

"One day I'll go back," she vowed to herself. "This nightmare has got to end sometime."

She was humming to herself as she entered the living room and took her usual seat, the one dead center of the two-seater sofa. She flicked through her book till she located the latest entry and placed the book on her lap so it lay across her knees, like an open invitation. Or challenge.

Jet entered the room without her journal. Rachael scowled. When would Jet grasp the importance of these sessions? Her life depended on them, whether she realized it or not.

Ben was the next to arrive. He, too, took his usual seat, the armchair that faced the mirror. He, too, was without his journal.

Rachael cast a nervous eye over each of them. Had they planned this together? Were they adding new secrets to old secrets till they became King and Queen of an unmanageable pile of secrets? Did they get a kick from treating these sessions as if they were a game?

Her fists curled into balls. She was acting irrationally, still, they were to blame for bursting her bubble of goodness and for that they had to be held accountable.

She forced her tone to be light. "Where is your journal, Ben?"

"I'm not up to Group today, Rach. Let's face it. Your type of therapy isn't working. How long have I been here? I'm still the same as the day I arrived."

Jet, slumped across the armchair with her leg hanging over the edge, looked like the poster child for incorrect posture. She began tapping her foot in the air. "I agree with Ben. We should skip the whole Group thing and relax. To think, I could be failing my final exams right now. Instead, I'm on vacation."

Rachael opened her mouth to remind Jet this wasn't supposed to be fun but Ben cut her off. "This is going to sound all boring and grown up, but you do realize your exams will be there when you get back?"

Jet gave him a wink. "You're not the only one who can block things out."

"I guess I'll go first," said Rachael, although she was sure she could have burst into flames and neither of them would have cared. Or noticed.

Ben and Jet were making silly faces at each other the way they had the first day. And like that first day, Rachael had to fight against the suctioning pull of the sofa. As she flicked through the book in her lap, disappointed that her joy was short lived, she began to fidget with restlessness. Nothing in her journal was impressive enough to be read out loud.

Damn it. Their negative vortex had completely derailed her. She lifted her head when she felt the ill wind that had resonated off the albino girl in the art room blow into the living room, settling on her like a mist, pressing against her chest, weighing her down. Yesterday, her words had seemed beautiful and inspiring, the works of a creative genius. Today, they were as uninteresting as the ingredients panel on a cereal box.

She searched for another passage. And another. Still nothing stood out as inspirational. Every page she skimmed, she discarded as drivel. How had every word in her book become a lie? Her hands shook but she forced herself to remain calm. "This is something that should lift our moods." She read:

"We all fall down sometimes. The trick is to keep getting back up. Hope can lift us when we feel as though we are stuck."

"Big deal," said Jet. "Coffee and alcohol can do the same thing. What else you got?"

Jet opened her mouth and patted it twice with her fingers in a mock yawn and Rachael pursed her lips as she searched her journal. One passage stood out. It seemed appropriate to their mood although she was reluctant to share it. It had a dark undertone that embarrassed her, and she was even more surprised that it was in her journal. Had she not recognized the scrawls as her own, she would have sworn someone was making secret entries. Besides, she had nothing else to share.

"Jet, you once asked me to hold my judgment about your views on God. Please do the same for me while I read this poem. I wrote it while trying to empathize with Ben."

Rachael forced back the tremor that wanted to creep into her voice:

"Put a candle on my back, let it burn until my fingers curl, I only need legs to run from this place. Put a chain around my neck, let it bend my head till it breaks off, I keep losing my mind anyway. Mirror don't you look at me. And I won't look at you—"

She stopped. The hairs along her neck were standing on end. She sensed the others were silently spurring her on but she was afraid.

Her words stuck in her throat. Her face dissolved into a waterfall of tears until she could no longer see the pages in her journal. "Oh, this is hopeless. I'm a complete failure."

Jet was looking at her with warmth and sincerity. "No, you're not. That was a very brave piece. It's full of honesty and pain. Not sure what any of it means exactly, but it's the most real I've seen you." She reached out a consoling hand.

Rachael jumped onto the sofa, balancing herself precariously on the arms. "Don't touch me."

"I forgot. Sorry. Really I am."

"Just don't touch me."

"Okay. I promise." Jet paused. "Do you want to come down from there and talk about it?"

Of course she wanted to talk about it. She was like a publicity hound desperately wanting to shed all her secrets. She was dying to tell them how she felt invisible all the time and how only through these sessions did she find peace.

Instead she bowed her head. "I wish I could."

"Does this have something to do with why you stopped believing in God? It's not my cup of tea, but I understand how some people need that level of faith."

Rachael jerked her head. Was that it? Was she glum because she'd lost her faith? Not just in God, but in herself? Was she scared she was going to end up like the girl in the art room who was passing color-by-number judgment on herself?

Leaping off the sofa, Rachael sprinted out of the room, ignoring their cries for her to come back. She had to get away, but where could she go?

She had nowhere to go. She'd never had anywhere to go. She'd just followed everyone, bounding along like a true follower.

Chapter Twelve

Jet waited till she heard the loud bang of the front door slamming shut.

"Good riddance to you," she sang out. "And while you're at it, have a good think about what a hypocrite you are." She turned to Ben. "Can you believe Rachael has the audacity to harass us into talking about our problems, yet the second it's her to turn to talk, she goes off like a spoiled brat? You know something? I'm sick to death of her almighty attitude."

Ben's eyes were closed and his head was propped up with a cushion. Fast asleep or zoned out, Jet envied him this ability to switch off from the surrounding world in the blink of an eye. With no other distractions on hand—TV, internet or cell phone—she found herself reliving her nightmarish reality over and over. Some days her guilt never let up.

His dreamy, faraway expression made him look cuter than hell. She smiled, reckoning she should be thankful that Rachael had run off, leaving Jet the chance to be alone with him. The pool incident had certainly proven he liked her.

She watched as his eyelashes fluttered with each rise and fall of his chest. An idea began to form in her mind. One so brilliant it sent a delicious shiver up her spine and she had to clamp her hand over her mouth to stop from squealing aloud. Even now, her skin began to tingle as she recalled the way his eyes had traveled up and down her body. If only the ghosts in the pool hadn't freaked her out. Who knew how far she and Ben might've gone?

Suddenly her stomach tightened, reminding her of another time she'd gone too far. But she cast this memory away. Ben was nothing like Lucas.

Still, she needed to be absolutely certain he was asleep and not pretending before she tried anything. He might ruin her surprise, and what if she never got a second chance? She leaned over the coffee table and waved her hands in front of his face. Not a flicker of movement, not even when she leant in close enough to see the tiny buds of stubble poking out on his chin.

"Should I even be doing this?" she whispered.

Her head said no, but her heart disagreed. As if both were fighting for control, her breathing started to come in quick, sharp bursts like air was escaping out of a balloon.

What harm could one little kiss do?

She stifled a giggle. The butterflies in her stomach were totally flipping out. Her inner voice egged her on, telling her this was the most romantic thing she would ever do in her life. No need to flip a coin. Her head lost, her heart won.

She held her breath. An image of someone else's lips crossed her vision. No. This was definitely *not* the same as kissing Lucas. She leaned in, closer now, a little bit closer still. Her eyes narrowed and her lips parted of their own accord as though bracing for the soft, moist touch of his mouth against hers. She was almost kissing him.

Jet pressed her lips firmly on his.

His eyes flew open.

This was it. No turning back.

What the—?

Something was digging into her throat, stuck as if she'd swallowed a piece of gravel.

Her heart began slamming inside her chest, banging

against the inside of her rib cage like a terrified bird on a one-way trip into a mineshaft.

The expression 'be still my beating heart' shouldn't have felt this painful.

She wrenched her eyes open to see that Ben had his nose pressed up against hers. His face was purple and contorted in hatred.

She struggled to breathe and it took her a moment to register that his hands were around her throat.

Oh my God, he's strangling me! Why is he strangling me?

She opened her mouth to suck down precious air, but her throat was closed. Not even the smallest gap for oxygen to get in.

She clawed at his hands, scratching him with her nails. But he was strong. So strong.

Help. Can't breathe.

At last she remembered to bang her fists as hard as she could against his face. Punching him, desperate to pull out of his hold, she might as well have bashed him with a strand of wool.

She grew weak. Her life faded from her and she was dragging down, down into the blackness. *It's me,* she tried to scream, but the effort only made her throat burn even more.

Near death, her chin fell to her shoulders.

Third time really was the charm.

But I don't want to die. Why did I ever think I did?

The essence of her life dimmed and everything started to fade away, leaving behind a solitary red dot.

One final thought flickered through her mind before she blacked out.

I'm too young to die.

* * *

Hours, or even days passed until oxygen was funneled into her mouth. Air began to fill her lungs and she could breathe again. Yeah, she could breathe, but her back hurt from falling onto the coffee table when Ben had let go.

At least she was alive.

Someone was screaming the same phrase over and over, "What have I done?"

Even temporarily blinded she saw Ben sobbing into his hands and rambling about ghosts. Her vision pulsed between shades of black and gray, finally settling on a motley pattern like she'd been staring into the sun. She opened her eyes a smidge. Despite trying to avoid looking at Ben, she did anyway. His face was a mixture of shock and revulsion. Tears were streaming down his cheeks. She tried to summon an ounce of empathy for him and found she lacked the desire.

Even though her lungs were working fine, she had trouble finding her voice.

The words came out in short gasps. "You tried to kill me."

"I felt someone pull my hands away," he spluttered. "You've got to believe me. I saw a light. Then someone was pulling at my hands." An eerie and distant pitch had crept into his voice, as though a spirit or alien presence was talking through him.

Jet sucked deeply on fresh air. With her throat still raw and bruised, she began coughing.

Ben held out his hands, palms facing up. His green eyes became reptilian as they searched the room for something only he could see.

"Ghosts," he shouted. "I saw them running after Jet. But they weren't going to hurt her. They were trying to save her. They were saving her from me!" He turned his attention to his hands, horror spreading across his face.

Her throat fully recovered, she shouted at him. "You're a freak, Ben Taylor. I don't ever want to speak to you again."

He snapped out of his daze. "No, don't say that. You're all I have left in this world."

"Well, you almost killed all you have left in this world."

"I can't hurt you. Don't you see? It was the ghosts. They'll do anything to stop me from harming you." He reached out a hand to touch her face.

She swatted him away. "Get away from me. Get away from me!"

"I would never hurt you. Jet, I love you."

"Well, I hate you. Go to hell!"

Her words seemed to have had the same effect as if she'd flung knives at him. He fell to his knees and clutched at his chest. And as much as she wanted to flee, she stood and watched as he fell to the floor. Unable to deal with the guilt and hurt, she buried her head in the cushions and bawled her eyes out, all the while cursing her mother and father for abandoning her, cursing Lucas for everything else, cursing Ben for showing her his dark side.

Ben revealing his dark side to her was what hurt her most.

Chapter Thirteen

His hands burned. Scalding hot like he'd plunged them into a nest of fire ants. Running his hands under cold water did nothing to ease the pain; it only seemed to spread the heat throughout his body.

What did you do this time, Ben? asked the little bug in his head. There no concern in its voice, only malice.

"Stop judging me," Ben growled, punching his reflection in the mirror.

The glass splintered, but not enough to break. He twisted his lips into a grin. All he needed was one piece of jagged glass and his nightmare of a life would end.

The bathtub. I could fill it up and go to sleep and this would all be over.

"Why didn't I think of it before?"

Just as quickly as the idea entered his head it disappeared, and Ben was left standing at the basin and running his hands under the faucet wondering what the hell had happened.

One second he was floating on a black river, dark and quiet as though he was in a sensory deprivation tank, and the next second he was dragged under the surface. Under the water, his mother was sitting in a chair, gazing out a window. He'd tried to swim to her but something bumped into him and pushed him off course. When he looked for his attacker, he saw a dead body floating by. Pushing the corpse out of the way, he spun around to find his mom, but in the black water he lost all sense of direction. Dead bodies were all around, bobbing up and down with their arms held out wide as if they were ghastly puppets desperate to embrace their undead puppet master.

Death did not frighten Ben. The inability to reach his mother did. He grabbed at the nearest body and flung it aside. Except that his hands wrapped around its lifeless neck…

His gut told him he hadn't gripped the neck of a corpse, but the soft, and very much alive flesh of the woman he hadn't realized he loved until now.

He'd nearly killed Jet.

Revulsion shuddered through him and he vomited. Watching his puke running down the sink, he wished he could follow.

The little bug inside his head was laughing and pointing at him. It disappeared into a tunnel for a second and reappeared with a sign that read OH BOY, SHE REALLY HATES YOU NOW.

No sense arguing with that logic.

Jet had every reason to hate him. Yet he wondered how many others were out there with hatred in their hearts for him. He'd seen terrible things, and done nothing to prevent them from happening, maybe even committed terrible acts himself.

He was only good for killing.

But would he have killed her?

Reliving every gory detail of his assault on Jet, he paused to reflect that a forceful presence had seemed to tug at his hands. As if someone or something had stopped him strangling her by prying apart his hands. The force had displayed enough power to unlock his grip that he should have seen bruises on his wrists.

He pushed up the sleeves of his shirt. No scars, nothing but a heavy, heady stench of the ocean. He turned his hands over and over, determined to see the telltale purple discoloration of a bruise forming.

If he saw no signs of bruising he might be able to convince his brain that *his* will had saved her life.

Nice try, but not a chance, said the little bug in his head. *Something* else *stopped you killing that girl. Which means* you *would have killed her.*

He turned the faucet so hard it almost snapped off in his hands. He wiped his palms on his pants till the skin was red and burned like hell. They'd probably burn forever. He prayed they would shrivel to a crisp and fall off. His hands were instruments of death. More lives would be spared. Let them fall off.

Without the water running to block out the sounds from the living room, he could clearly hear Jet howling. Icicles pierced his heart knowing he was the cause of her tears. The son of a religious man, kindness was as much a part of his daily meal as potatoes. He wasn't used to people hating him.

He tiptoed into the living room. "Jet?"

"Go to hell!"

He would have kissed the Devil himself if it would have earned him her forgiveness, but he would have to settle for finding Rachael. She would help him fix this latest mistake. Although her advice would probably be to tell him to record the experience in his journal, but how could he? If he wrote it down, it would be true. And more than anything he wanted to erase this particular moment from his mind. He'd managed to erase the six months of the war. Surely sticking a Band-Aid over this memory would have the same effect.

With me around, you'll never forget, the little bug in his head told him.

"I'm warning you," he shouted. "Get out of my mind." Seething with anger, he butted his head against the wall so hard the plasterboard cracked.

* * *

He found Rachael in a room he'd never noticed before. The door was open and Rachael was sitting amid an art group. Creative appreciation was something he never understood, preferring to admire mountains, rivers and trees firsthand. A piece of cloth failed to capture the scent of a log fire, the pelt of rain or the slap of a tide. Maybe he had never set foot in this room before, but he hated it like it was a torture chamber.

As he stepped into the room he was cringing. Through tight lips he sneered, "If someone asks me if I want a mocha latte I'm going to punch the living hell out of them."

He clenched his fists to prove it.

The room was quiet, which wasn't surprising. What was unusual was the temperature, freezing cold. And the room was bright, giving him an insight into what the insides of Superman's crystal cave might feel like.

Caves were usually filled with other things too, like bats, golems, dragons and other monsters that were sometimes nothing more than fanciful wanderings of the mind. Sometimes they were real. This room was bright and filled with something else entirely creepy, though he couldn't see or hear it. One word echoed in his mind. *Abyss.* With no end to the whiteness, this room seemed to grow and shrink with each step. He'd read enough of his father's Bible to know an abyss was the dwelling place of demons.

He shook himself free of the idea and took another step toward Rachael, although he was halted by the sight of a tall, pale shape floating toward him. Ben was hypnotized by the ghostly shape, which he recognized as a girl, strikingly similar to the shadows in the mirror.

Had the images that had plagued him since day one at last come to life? As the shadow-girl glided toward him he saw bright lights ricocheting off the white walls. For a second he imagined she was on inline skates beneath a giant mirror ball.

Shadow-girl skated to her right and stopped in front of Rachael. Then she leaned in close, drawing the surrounding white storm with her. Mist swirled around the two girls as though they were trapped inside a tornado, but neither of them looked scared.

"Come paint with us," said a voice directly behind him.

Ben jumped. When he spun, he was face to face with another pale shadow-girl. Close up, she was beautiful and ugly at the same time. Hypnotic yet repulsive. Light and dark. Ben wanted to flee, yet he also wanted to embrace her. Instinct screamed that something was wrong with this girl.

He fought to shake off the hypnotic spell. He was here to talk to Rachael. She would know how to fix his latest mistake.

Turning away from the shadow-girl he saw Rachael had become fully engulfed in the cloud of fog invading the room.

"Rachael." His lungs felt heavy. He called out louder. "Rachael!"

Whether or not she heard, the swirling bright light was fast swallowing her.

"Rachael!"

She looked at him. A euphoric look softened her features. His skin crawled. The shadow-girl had disappeared into the mist, but he sensed her evil was taking Rachael.

"Rachael! Get out of here."

He was worried that she couldn't sense the presence of wrongness in the room even though she was so intuitive. The evil was a presence that pulsed as strong as the light yet seemed masked by it. Or perhaps hiding within the light.

"Come paint with us, Ben Taylor," urged the voice again. And before he could ask how she knew his name, she vanished.

He ran out of the room as if enemy fire was gunning him down.

He ran till his chest burned. His record was two minutes at flat-out speed. He felt like time had slowed while he ran from the art room to the living room. Sprinting along a corridor, numberless doors on either side, grey carpet worn through, cracked paint on the walls.

Should he recognize this place?

Think.

Not only had the shadow-girl disturbed him, not only was he frightened that he couldn't identify his surroundings, but he was gripped by an anxiety attack. A silent, urgent call was coming from the mirror, and he had to get back to hear it.

When he returned to living room he fell into the armchair. A song floated on the air that only he could hear. He closed his eyes to bask in the song, and when he next opened them Rachael sat on the sofa.

How long had dozed off for?

Humming, she wore a secretive smile on her face. That alone alerted Ben to the seriousness of her adventure in the art room. Plus she looked happy. Rachael was never happy. Her eyes carried a haunted, heartbroken expression. Now they were shining, though not from laughter the way Jet's eyes had.

Alarm bells rang inside Ben's head. With absolute certainty he could vow she had *always* taken the middle seat of the sofa and she had *always* placed her journal on her lap, open and ready for Group. Now she was curled up with her feet neatly tucked behind her knees.

Her state of relaxed euphoria and the fog he had seen in the art gallery had to be related.

"Have you been smoking marijuana?" he asked.

She ignored him, which made him clench his teeth. *Damned hippie artists.* Maybe strangling Jet was an accident, but if Rachael had taken drugs he'd leave no doubt that her death was intentional.

"Rachael!"

"No."

"Because you know that stuff is bad for you."

"You've smoked it."

His back stiffened. "Listen, kiddo. What you and I do are two different things."

"You are so right about that," she muttered.

"Maybe it's time I started looking after you."

"No need to worry yourself. I'm fine. But you and Jet had better sort yourselves out real quick. I'm not sure how much longer I can keep this charade up?"

What charade? Ben sat bolt upright. Concern filled him. Something was wrong. This wasn't the Rachael he knew. "Are you all right? I saw you with those drugged-up hippies. And now you're acting like a completely different person."

"Maybe this is who I really am." She opened one eye and

peered at him through her lashes.

He felt his face drain of color. "Stop it, Rach. You're scaring me."

"Welcome to my world."

He'd heard enough crazy talk. He stood up and stormed out of the room, determined to track down the asshole who was dealing drugs. His heart rate began climbing at the prospect of doing damage. Not only was he trained to cause damage, somewhere along the way it had become fun. He found himself lifting his lips in a sneer. No wonder he was in a psych hospital.

Chapter Fourteen

The front door slammed. Jet decided her room offered more privacy so she lifted her exhausted body off the couch and staggered along the hall till she flopped onto the bed.

Despite her mental fatigue, her body was restless. She tossed this way, turned that way, got up, got back up from the bed and laid back down again.

Then she was back up and in front of her dresser mirror, fiercely wanting the day to be over. It seemed to be dragging on the way a hot, windless day did. She tried blotting the memory of Ben strangling her out of her mind, the way she might have tried ignoring snide remarks in school, but an hour later her throat was still stinging and her pride even more so.

She closed her eyes. She wished she could abandon her curiosity, because if her neck was covered in bruises without a shadow of a doubt Ben had tried to strangle her.

Close your eyes and the mind will follow.

If only denial was that easy. She would have given anything for the past few weeks to be erased from her mind.

For the first time she truly wished she was at home. Nothing in this place was as she dreamt it would be. No loving parents, no caring doctors, no break from the constant reminder that her life was a mess. And her two companions in this private hellhole were a pesky know-it-all brat and a soldier who'd tried to kill her.

If only she could hate Ben, but the truth was, the feelings she had for him were stronger than anything she'd ever felt. After the way Lucas had treated her, she'd never expected her heart to stir for another guy.

Rubbing her neck, she told herself once more that for her own safety she needed to hate Ben.

She opened her eyes and counted at least four different purple marks on her neck. "Oh, who am I kidding? He should be locked up."

Opening the closet door and slamming it shut again, kicking clothes around the room out of frustration, she decided to calm her fierce mood with a walk. Yet after her experience at both the pool and the art room, the thought of leaving the sanctuary of her room brought on the shakes. So she spent the next few minutes pacing up and down the floor, cursing her parents for bringing her teddy bear instead of her CD player so she could lose herself in her favorite music.

"I need to figure out a way of avoiding Ben until I get released from this nut house," she told herself.

And it has to be an excuse plausible enough to fool my sanctimonious and nosy roommate, she added as an afterthought.

Hey Ben. The thing is I'm hormonal. Or how about? The thing is I'm radioactive. Or maybe? The thing is I'm an alien and my mother ship will be arriving any minute now and for your own safety we need to stay away from each other.

She suspected Rachael would see through any excuse to avoid Ben.

A shiver ran along her spine. Why did Rachael make her feel as if she should be confessing to something?

"Not that I've done anything wrong."

When she looked at her teddy bear, he seemed to be

judging her so she threw him into the closet.

She quit searching for a means of avoiding Ben when her right temple started throbbing. She laughed out loud. "Freakin' typical that I end up in a healing center with an antidrug policy."

She could rid herself of her pounding headache by lying down on the bed but she was afraid to go to sleep. What if the hatred she'd detected in Ben's eyes continued to haunt her sleeping mind as much as it haunted her waking moments? But sleep was her only escape now.

"Where are you, Mom?" she whispered as she pulled the blanket over her shoulders. "I really need your help."

* * *

Rarely did her father drive her to school but the bus drivers were on strike. It would have cost a fortune to take a taxi. And even if they did have a second car, her mother didn't drive. So her dad would drop her off to school on his way to work.

Embarrassed, she slouched low in the passenger seat and peered out of the window over its bottom rim as her dad pulled out onto the street. "How was Jakarta?"

"Boring," her dad replied. "Like I told you it would be."

A few blocks later he drove into a service station. When he'd disappeared inside to pay she'd opened every compartment on the chance that money was stashed somewhere. She came up empty-handed. However, wedged in the center console underneath a pile of parking receipts and a Johnny Cash CD was a brochure for a holiday resort in tropical North Queensland. The photo staring back at her was so classy it seemed to warrant that a butler trailed behind with a silver platter.

Maybe her scrooge of a father was planning a special family vacation, she thought.

She purposely banged her forehead against the car window to dislodge the fantasy. Yeah right. No way was *he* spending money on something this fancy. They'd be lucky if they got to drive by a shady trailer park.

Still, she couldn't tear her mind away from the idea of a family vacation. What other reason was there for the brochure to be in the car?

At times like this Jet wished she had a sibling to confide in.

She was about to slide the brochure back under the CD when something else caught her eye. On the inside sleeve of the brochure, in a thick red scrawl that looked remarkably like lipstick, was a telephone number. Beside the number was a drawing of a love heart.

Intrigued to the point of distraction, Jet stopped by a travel agent after school. She flipped through the racks until she found the same brochure as the one hidden in her dad's car. By the time she got home her sense of intrigue was replaced with a force to be reckoned with.

Revenge.

At last, she had the ammunition necessary to extract from him enough money to buy the red, backless dress for the school dance. Her life would be in ruins without that dress. And matching shoes. Yes, she would need shoes as well.

At dinner that evening, with the brochure wedged firmly between her thighs for moral support, she blurted out, "Dad, I want a new dress for the school dance."

Damn it. I forgot to mention the shoes.

"Julliet!" Her mother's face had turned twenty shades redder than the tomatoes in her salad.

"Now, listen here." Her father put down his cutlery and smoothed his hands on the tablecloth.

Here we go, she thought. Here comes his masterfully perfected lecture face. Which means he either wants Mom to chaperone me to the dance or he wants me home by nine. That was okay. She could negotiate the conditions.

"You're not going to the prom."

"What!"

He matched her shout with a loud thump on the table and for a second she saw his cool resolve break away. But she refused to flinch. His stern demeanor returned and he stared at her with condescension in his eyes. She ached to throw her juice in his face.

"I know what goes on at those dances. First a boy spikes the punch and the next thing he and his friends are taking advantage of the girls in any dark corner they can find—"

"That's not true. Mom! Tell him that's not true."

Her mother refused to meet her heated gaze. Instead she seemed to be engrossed in the pattern on the tablecloth.

"Then one of the boys will tell you they have a hotel suite booked so the party can carry on. Only when you get there is no party and you find yourself alone with the boy. Or worse yet, and this is every father's nightmare, my dear child, you'll be alone with a group of boys."

"That won't happen. I would never do that. Mom, tell him I would never do that."

Her mother was now tracing the pattern in the cloth with her finger. Great ally she turned out to be.

Her father glared at her and she swore she saw glee in his eyes. "I know it won't. Because you're banned from attending the school dance. And that's final."

Rage propelled off her chair. Rage also rendered her mute. All she could manage was a seething glare that flared her nostrils in and out, followed by a heavy foot-stomping session that took her out of the room. At the bottom of the stairs, she stopped and placed the travel brochure on the hall table in a spot where her father would have to have been blind not to see it, right under his car keys. He would also have to be stupid to miss the subtle hint.

Biting her lip, she considered going back into the dining room to accuse him of cheating on her mother. But what if her mother was unaware of the affair? What a horrible way to find out.

"It would serve her right, though," she snarled as she ran up the stairs, ignoring her father's orders that she come back and finish her dinner.

She slammed the door to her room. Despite her anger, she would never hurt her mother so cruelly by advertising her father's indiscretions at the dinner table.

"As much as I hate that stupid cow right now, I will never be like him," she told the teddy bear on her bed.

Teddy sat quietly, as he always did when she was in a mood. He even stayed quiet when she spent a further five minutes wildly kicking at the clothes on her floor for no reason other than she was mad.

A few moments later, Lucas sent her a text message:
party 2nite wana go

Of course she wanted to go. Her parents were ruining her life and she was itching to get out of the house.

She turned to face the dresser mirror, smiling, but not a shred of warmth was in that smile. It radiated spite worthy of a serial killer and was a wonderful accessory for her current mood. There would be liquor at this party, and more than anything in the world she wanted to get totally smashed. And she would do so on whatever mind-bending beverage she could get her hands on.

"I'll lick a freshly painted wall to get high right now," she said, tossing her teddy bear off the bed so she could get to her clothes. Her laugh was cold and cruel. "That would really shit him."

This party would be her first nighttime social gathering that wasn't exclusively made up of her relatives. Not that she was worried about anything going wrong, though. She'd be with Lucas. Her father was overreacting to think all men wanted one thing from a girl.

A stabbing pain hit her chest. She was mostly upset with her father because he'd passed judgment on Lucas and his friends without having met them. Her father carried on as if every male wanted to rape her. Lucas and his friends weren't like that at all.

Her inner voice reminded her she'd only known Lucas and his friends for two months so was she really the best judge of their characters?

Who cared? Tonight was about liberation. She was going to be free of his shackles forever. But first she'd have to escape the house without getting caught.

She replied to the text message, telling Lucas she'd meet him around the corner in ten minutes. With no time to spare she squeezed her hands under the mattress till she touched something slippery. She pulled out a glittery, strapless top, which matched with the next item of clothing she retrieved, a pair of designer jeans that Lucas had bought for her birthday. The black ballerina shoes she slipped onto her feet were hers.

Flats were essential for her escape route, which was out her parents' bedroom window and across the tiled roof of the patio area below, where she made a blind leap into a flower bed.

Precisely nine and one-half minutes later, Jet was sliding into a black Honda, kissing Lucas passionately on the lips, then picking dead flowers out of her hair. She also flicked off whatever guilt had managed to find its way into her. After all, her parents had kept secrets from her since before she was born. Deception ran in the Jones household like mice from a cat.

Chapter Fifteen

Ben snapped out of sleep when someone called his name. His army-honed reflexes kicked in and he was up off the bed, reaching for his M-247. For a split second he thought he was in the Iraqi desert with orange flares exploding across the night sky. Momentarily blinded, he spun about the room searching for his gun, but he knocked over the bedside lamp and a half-filled cup of coffee.

Behind him came the repetitive boom of an AK-47. Enemy fire.

Damn it. Where's my gun?

His body recoiled as a jolt of reality switched his mind on, and he realized he wasn't hearing gunfire. Someone was banging on his bedroom door.

"Open up. Quick. I have to talk to you."

Jet? Relief flooded through him. He almost knocked out his teeth as he crashed into the door in his haste to open it. As he opened the door he seemed to have forgotten that he was half-naked.

Jet's face was riddled with worry. "Rachael's missing. You have to help me look for her."

"Did she say she was going anywhere?" he asked, throwing on his shirt and following her along the corridor.

"No. I just woke up and she wasn't in the room. I went looking for her in the living room but she's not there either."

"It's not like her to be missing."

Rachael was normally a permanent fixture in the living room, and Ben had to see it for himself to believe Jet. Sure enough, Rachael was missing. Luckily there were few other places she could be, and they soon found her in the art gallery.

Ben hesitated as he stood in the doorway. What if the shadow-girl was inside, only this time she was going to force him to stay until he painted something? He'd grown up in a household where hitting girls was unacceptable, yet the shadow-girl had terrified him so badly he was prepared to punch the daylights out of her.

Jet seemed oblivious to the chill that hung in the air as she pushed past him.

Alone in the room, Rachael sat in front of an easel. She wasn't painting, though. She was staring at a blank canvas while gripping a paintbrush with such force her knuckles threatened to burst through the skin.

"Rach?" He coughed to stop his voice from trembling. "What are you doing here?"

"You tell me. I haven't got a clue and I'm supposed to know everything." Her voice was barely above a low whisper. Her eyes were wild, her cheeks glistening with either sweat or tears.

"Come back to bed. It's too late to be running around," Ben told her.

"Do I look like I'm running around?"

"No. You look like you're waiting for the bus."

"Well, I'm not."

"What are you doing then?"

"Hiding out."

His voice tightened. "Is somebody after you?"

She shook her head. "That's not why I'm here. Do you ever get tired of pretending everything is fine when it's clearly not?" She let out a harsh laugh.

Ben cringed. He'd never heard such fear in a voice before, not even his own.

"What am I saying?" she cackled. "There's nothing wrong with me. You two are the ones with the problem. I shouldn't even be here."

She was still gripping the paintbrush tightly. He was afraid it would snap in two. An image of her stabbing the jagged end into her arm flashed across his vision.

Why did he always have to see life in gruesome detail? A chill crept under his skin and he tried to shake it off, even though he believed that the evil presence he'd felt earlier was returning. "Maybe you have a point. You shouldn't be here but none of us should. We should vow never to come in this room again."

"You got my vote," Jet said.

"Whatd'ya say, Rach? Let go of the paintbrush so we can get out of here."

She turned the brush over in her hand, as though seeing it for the first time. "Do you get the feeling we're going to end up trapped in this place forever? I do."

"Come back to bed. You scribble all day in your journal. You're obviously exhausted." Jet took a step forward.

Rachael leaped out of the chair. She flew behind the easel to hide and began screaming, "Stay away from me!"

"Damn it, I forgot again." Jet backed away. "Come on. Please. You'll be safe with us."

She glanced over at Ben, who shrugged his shoulders. Ordinarily he would have agreed, but even with his army training, he wasn't sure if he could defend himself against the evil presence in the room. But he was damned if he'd leave Rachael here a second longer. He made beckoning signals with his hands as though coaxing her out from a hiding place.

Like a frightened puppy she responded. "None of us is safe," she wailed.

She could protest all she wanted, so long as she moved toward the exit.

Jet, too, was gesturing, beckoning. "As long as we stick together we'll be safe. Soldier Boy will protect us. Right?"

"Of course I will."

Liar.

Rachael sighed and let her head fall onto her chest. But at least she was following their lead, even if she was shaking with fear. "It won't matter. I'm going to end up here so I might as well learn to paint. It's so unfair. I don't belong here." She let out a heart-wrenching sob.

"None of us wants to be here," Ben muttered.

Rachael shook her head. "You don't understand. I don't belong here. Unlike you two."

He let her remark slide because she was almost to the door. He prayed the invisible lead held. The little bug in his head began to question why she was excluding herself in the mess they were in together. For once he agreed with the little bug in his head.

Jet raised her hand. "Hey, I have a brilliant idea for Group tomorrow. How about I tell you something so fantastic you'll be able to analyze me for years? And after I spill my guts we promise to get things back to the way they were before we came to this stupid place. Maybe we can be better than before. We weren't born damaged, you know."

"Jet has a point," Ben said. "We can get well enough to leave this place. We just have to make the effort."

"And once we're free we'll remain best friends," Jet added.

Ben wished that were the case. Call it a hunch, but he

doubted he'd see any of them again once this nightmare was over.

As Rachael followed them out of the gallery, he stopped. He thought he heard someone hissing at him. At the doorway the lights shone brightly and he was sure a frail, pale hand swiped out at him and scratched his cheek.

But later, when he stood in front of the bathroom mirror to check his face, instead of seeing scratch marks he saw something else. The mirror in the bathroom was misted with the same white shadows that haunted the mirror in the living room.

* * *

Ben stayed outside in the hall while Rachael tucked herself into bed. Jet popped her head out the door, yawned, and told him she was going to bed as well. He was too wired to contemplate sleep so he went to the living room, sat on the sofa, and stared at the shadows in the mirror. He found comfort in routine. This evening, though, something was different.

Typically, the living room was dark at night, yet now a glow was emanating from the walls and ceiling. Perhaps a full moon explained the stingray-like pale shapes that were clinging to the cornices.

The shapes moved.

Impossible. Shadows moved only when the host moved. But if shadows were unable to move on their own, how had they spread from this mirror to the one in bathroom?

The shadows spoke to him.

"What do you want?"

Silence.

He cast the shadows out of his mind and focused instead on the pale shape that had haunted his every waking thought since he'd strayed into the art room He could have sworn the shadow-girl from the other day was the same shadow-girl who had taken a swipe at him tonight. He couldn't understand why she had attacked him. He'd done nothing to her.

Strange as the peculiar girl was, she also seemed familiar. He struggled to grasp it. The little bug in his head helped him figure it out by telling him to think about what was *un*familiar.

Good point. What was unusual about the girl? She had a pale complexion and to stare at her was akin to staring at the moon. Except that her complexion could be explained by a rare skin condition.

What about the way the shards of crystal light radiated *from* her, not *to* her, as though she was the source of light?

He glanced up at the ceiling. Nothing could explain the way the beams of light made her appear fragmented, as though she had an echo of illumination trailing behind her.

"She's a distortion of light. An optical illusion." He was momentarily surprised by this revelation.

Was there a sane inner voice trapped inside his head, too? Would it survive among the angry mob of voices? Or would it be eaten alive?

His head began to throb. Gripping his temples, he curled up on the sofa.

* * *

A house. Not mine because I live at home with my mother and kid sister. Mom keeps a tidy house. Washes and irons my clothes, cooks for me, lets me pretty much do what I like. The smell of freshly baked cake on a Sunday afternoon is what I miss the most. This house smells like someone painted the walls with gunpowder and the blood of dead animals. And what a mess. Not messy from clutter or clothes the way the floor looks on Christmas morning after everyone has finished unwrapping their presents. This home is untidy from rubble and debris.

The windows have big gaping holes in them, letting every sound and stench in from outside. Some of the walls are missing, too.

Someone's screaming. I see a man in a traditional white robe. His face is red from shouting at us to get out of his house. At least that's what our interpreter says the man is yelling.

A baby's screaming as well. As I look around I count seven children. Ages three and up. No baby, though I can hear its desperate cries for food, even over the noise of helicopters, bombs, and gunfire outside.

The cries are coming from behind a table. Slowly inching myself onto the tips of my boots, I see the top of a head wrap. Belongs to the woman of the household. She rocks her baby back and forth to quiet it.

Does she know I can see her?

I don't blame her for hiding. We come bearing bad news. The man is told by our interpreter to pack up his family and their things and get out. Where will they go, he shouts? Outside, the sergeant tells him. Is the sergeant crazy? A blind man can see it's a war zone out there…

Guns are going off and as I run for cover I hold my arms out wide so a stray bullet might hit me and send me home or to the hospital. I don't care which. Desperation makes me hope for a bullet to pass through the cheaply made flak jacket, which offers no protection to any of my vital organs. I want this stint in hell to be over. Why did I come?

Sergeant says we lose a month's pay if we try to get killed intentionally. So the trick is to do it properly, get a bullet in the head, or a main artery in the arm or leg. But most of the guys here are such poor shots, we have more chance of getting our Johnsons shot off than going home in a casket.

Realizing the gunfire is from M-16s, our guns, I stop running. Let them get me. Let them do whatever they like to me. I'm over this war.

The earth around me is quiet. The sun has shifted. Time has sped up, and I've lost a few hours. Body bags are getting dragged to the shack at the front of the military compound. Curiosity makes me want to ask whether it's soldiers or civilians in the bags, but we don't ask questions around here. Not if we know what's good for us. I've already been stripped of all rank and docked a thousand bucks for speaking up against an attack on a mentally handicapped man. He was being beaten to death because he spoke funny. Who do we think we are to administer cruelty instead of aid?

Never mind, I tell the soldier who stares at me like he wants to kill me for caring about human life. I don't need to know who's ended up inside the bags. The rule is, kill a civilian and it's us who takes responsibility for the body until a relative can come and claim it. With sickening dread I know that if it's our side who's wrapping dead civilians into bags, it's our side who's putting them there.

* * *

Ben woke up drenched in sweat and shivering with a fear that glaciated him. This was worse than his usual nightmares, which he willed to return rather than accept that his memories had finally come home to haunt him. And they seemed to be striking with such vengeance that the sutures that had kept his sanity in place were tearing apart. Something more damaging than blood would flow when the wound reopened because his head was filled with toxic poison.

And the truly scary part was than nobody stuck inside his personal kill zone was safe.

Chapter Sixteen

Early the next morning, Rachael walked into the living room and saw a stranger standing over by the window. She let out a tiny squeal and tucked herself behind an armchair. This was the second time someone had shown up unannounced.

"The administration in this place is appalling," she muttered.

In two strides the stranger filled the gap between the balcony door and her chair, and extended his hand to her. Instead of running, which is what she usually did whenever anyone came too close, her feet were frozen to the floor.

"Hey. I'm Neale." He thrust his hand in her face.

Jet was suddenly at Rachael's side. She took a step toward Neale as though bracing for a fight. "She hates anyone touching her."

His eyes lit. Recognition?

Jet eyed him with skepticism. "Are you a doctor?" she asked, giving him a look up and down. "It's about time you showed up."

"He's too young to be a doctor," Rachael said.

Neale whipped his hand back and ran it through his hair as if he'd meant to do that from the start. "My dad runs this place. He's forcing me to hang here as an observer. I think he wants me to take over one day or something. Anyway, you should act normal and pretend like I'm not here."

Ben entered the room and shot a hostile stare in Neale's direction. Rachael was taken aback, but then Ben must have realized Neale posed no threat to him because he zigzagged his way to his favorite chair and resumed his daily ritual of mirror-gazing.

"At least one of us will find it easy to pretend you're invisible." Jet said with a smirk.

"Am I interrupting something?" Neale asked. His disarming smile twitched slightly, yet his eyes remained alert. He had an uncanny ability of focusing his attention on all three of them at once.

Rachael found him unnerving. "We were just about to start Group."

"Group?"

Sighing, she reached inside her jacket and pulled out her diary, and from the drawer of the coffee table she retrieved a blank journal. When Jet had showed up Rachael had been pleased to explain the fundamentals of Group. Today, she couldn't muster up any enthusiasm for the therapy session so she slid the blank journal across the coffee table toward Neale without explanation.

"We write down our thoughts and feelings and afterwards we discuss them," Jet said. "It's how we work on getting better."

Neale smiled. "Can I write song lyrics? I have loads of ideas in my head."

"You can write whatever you want," Jet answered.

"He said he was here as an observer," Rachael said, eyeing him warily.

Jet shrugged her shoulders and linked her arm through Neale's. "What does it matter why he's here? As long as he is, he may as well join in. Shall we start Group?"

Rachael retrieved her journal and pressed it close to her chest. Neale's sudden appearance spooked her. Worse, he avoided eye contact like he was hiding something. Only through writing in her journal would the volley of thoughts inside her head settle. Only with a clear mind would she make sense of his presence.

A devout participant in Group, she was suddenly afraid.

"I have something else I need to do right now," she said. "Do you mind if we postpone Group for a few hours?"

Jet's eyes widened, but she regained her composure and gave Rachael a sympathetic nod. "Sure, if that's what you want, Rach, fine by me." Jet turned to face Neale, beaming. "Hey, if your dad runs this place you must have the keys to the wine bar. I'm bored out of my freakin' mind."

* * *

Rachael—Journal entry

I had suggested writing in a journal as an exercise to awaken Ben's deeply repressed memories. I figured, if he had trouble talking about his past he could write about it instead. I had no idea that I'd end up using the journal to record my own feelings.

Strange to even admit I have them. As a messenger of God, I am bound to do His work as instructed and without so much as a shred of opinion or judgment.

In this way, Ben and I are similar. We are both soldiers sent to do the bidding of a higher commander and as such, rarely have we been privy to the big picture. Like contestants in a game show we are given one clue at a time. Faith keeps us pressing the buzzer.

Even though faith is blind, we were blinder. We should have demanded to know the rules.

Rachael paused. Her hands were trembling. She'd never given any credence to the doubt that had crept into her mind scores of years before. Her uncertainty had always lain dormant until Ben's and Jet's pooled skepticism had finally awakened that repressed doubt. But where had this reservation initially come from?

She put pen to paper once more:

How can I begin to understand where my rebellious streak came from when I am not mortal? Never before have I had reason to question my orders.

She clicked the top of her pen once more. That wasn't entirely true. Over the centuries she had held the role of guardian angel to hundreds of mortals. She had seen them born, live either well or poorly, then die. Life and death were absolute. Often she had hidden her alarm at how some mortals suffered terribly while others went about life without apparent effort.

Her pen ran across the page once again:

Mortals blossom like plants and return to the soil. God created them that way. They cannot escape nor cheat death, though countless have tried. They all meet the same fate. The question is this: Am I getting the chance to help put an end to one mortal's suffering?

She stopped. Clarity struck her as sharply as a bell's chime. Ben would stay in Purgatory forever unless she broke the rules. And the thought of her beloved mortal trapped anywhere except Heaven terrified her. Her head swam as the terror of his fate became apparent.

Taking a deep breath, she clicked her pen and returned to writing in her journal:

The appearance of Jet threw me into a wing spin. Ben and I were alone together for so long that at first I suspected her of being a spy. Yet she definitely has the fragile aura of a mortal so it's easy to rule her out as one of us.

At the start I resented her presence here. Good heavens, is it resentment I feel? Or am I simply channeling human emotions because I've spent centuries with them? Has my empathy evolved to become my behavior? Why do I have no one to ask?

No matter. I've seen the way she interacts with Ben, which is helping. Goodness me, I should be thankful she's here, not bitter. Great. Even my gratitude is begrudging.

Seriously. What is wrong with me? I should not *be feeling jealousy or impatience or* anything. *I am not human! The fact remains that Jet is in Purgatory, too, and I'll have to accept that she needs my help to ascend, but only after Ben has departed.*

And then there's Neale, an enigmatic mystery who has ruffled more than a few of my feathers. My brain is consumed with wondering why he's appeared. He is definitely one of my kind. And a rather high ranking one at that.

Maybe I'm under review, although I doubt that's the reason he's here. I would know if there was such a thing as a review process. Still, a high-ranking angel appears immediately after the biggest failure of my career. Coincidence? There is no such thing.

Now, if I only could see where I went wrong.

* * *

When Rachael looked up a little while later, Neale was smiling at her. She was momentarily blinded.

"So what did a nice girl like you do to end up here?" he asked.

Jet might have fallen for his charm, but his boyish good looks and perfect teeth were wasted on Rachael.

"Nothing. A bomb went off and my beloved mortal ended up in Purgatory. What I don't understand is how I got pulled in with him."

"At least you know where you are," Neale said.

"Where else would I be?"

Neale fidgeted. For a second Rachael wondered if he was hiding something. But that was impossible. Angels had no need to keep secrets from each other.

"Who are you and why are you here?" she asked, speaking to him in their ancient language.

Neale winced but seemed to get the point. He replied using the same tongue.

"I am Neale of the Ocean Winds. I know as much as you do, Rachael of the Winter Forests." He reverted back to a language the mortals understood. "But at least you know what I am. I was beginning to think my glimmer was so exceptional I could fool anybody, even an angel as old and wise as you."

"Shut up. I'm not that old."

He sighed. "I am. Anyway, you can relax. I'm not here to expose you. Jet and Ben will be none the wiser about your true identity. But I am here to tell you time is running out."

"I'm doing the best I can, given the circumstances."

His probing stare caused her face to flush with guilt.

"Look. I've never been locked in Purgatory before. Mortals die and it used to be the job of the living to pray for them so they'd find redemption and cross over. But there's one small problem. The living don't care about the dead anymore. The way I see it, angels are the new recruits helping lost souls ascend. At least, that's what I think. Why else was I pulled back?" She raised her eyebrows at him.

"Perhaps you'd care to elaborate?"

"I can't tell you what I don't know."

Rachael began pacing up and down the length of her bedroom while rubbing her hands together. "Let's put aside the feeling I have that you're holding out on me. I'm a big girl, I can figure this out. Obviously, Ben is refusing to remember specific details about the war. Without those memories he can never know why he needs forgiveness."

She gave him a questioning stare but his expression was unreadable. He folded his arms and said, "Go on."

So she figured she was on the right track. "I was there with him, watching everything that went on. But how can I ask him if he thinks witnessing a man get shot till his arm slices off has anything to do with his amnesia? Maybe I should remind him about the ten-year-old boy who curled up to his dying father's body because their car was two feet over an invisible border. His fellow countrymen orphaned an innocent boy. Surely his brain will get a zap from the realization."

"If only you could tell him all this," Neale muttered.

"Exactly." She was getting worked up, but she no longer cared. At least while Neale remained aloof she was able to ramble on. What a relief to finally have someone with whom she could discuss her problems.

"You know something, talking to you is really helping. I've spent my life conversing with mortals without any of them hearing me. They believe I am the wind or a cosmic force speaking to them." She cast her eyes upwards. "At long last, one of them is talking back. I've never felt this alive or significant. I only wish I could reveal myself to Ben because it would really move things along."

"You're forgetting one thing. You broke a rule when you developed a relationship with a mortal."

"Give me a break. How can I not form a relationship? What am I supposed to do? Hide in the crevices while Ben stumbles around getting crazier and crazier with every passing minute? He doesn't even know he's dead." Rachael stopped pacing and pointed a finger accusingly at Neale. "Whatever it takes to help him ascend, I'll do it."

"Your commitment is faultless."

She raised an eyebrow. "Like you'd tell me my flaws if you could. Anyway, my plan of getting Ben to record his dreams and feelings in a journal is brilliant. Why doesn't his journal hold the key to unlocking his memories? I've read the thing a thousand times and still nothing."

"If only Ben had the same inquisitive mind as you. If he would just snoop as low as to pry into your journal then all would be revealed and technically you wouldn't have broken the rule forbidding angels to reveal themselves to mortals." Neale gave her a mischievous smile.

Rachael scowled. "All right, so I have considered leaving my journal lying around where he can find it. Jet poses a slight problem, though. I doubt she'd hesitate about snooping. My issue isn't with her finding out who I really am. Believe me, pretending to be human is harder to pull off than you think. My issue is that I haven't figured out where she fits in to the puzzle."

"Would it bother you if Jet was the one who helped Ben ascend to heaven?"

"Of course not."

She realized this was a big fat lie. She reckoned Neale realized it, too.

He was watching her face with keen interest, or was it apprehension? She couldn't be sure.

"Human emotions are not ours to own or display," he said carefully. "It's not healthy for angels to mimic humans for too long."

"Oh, shut up about what's healthy for me. All I care about is helping Ben ascend."

"Jet seems to be having a positive impact on Ben. I see the way he looks at her."

Rachael nodded. "But something has happened. They used to make lovey-dovey faces at each other."

"Still, he is making progress. You may not hear it because you're so close to him, but I hear the cracks of his memory loosening."

She scoffed. "I think you're referring to the cracks in his mind. Neale, tell me how I'm supposed to help Ben when I have no clue?"

All the humor had disappeared from his face. "I can't help you there. But I do know that time is running out."

"Yes, so you've said."

As an angel she got to see the clocks that ticked for mortals. She'd also never lost a soul to hell and she wouldn't this time. She'd do whatever it took to help Ben ascend.

Chapter Seventeen

Rachael—Journal entry

Do angels have dreams? Night after night I watch their memories play out in my mind as clearly as if I was there when it happened. In Ben's case I was, nevertheless I'm still struck speechless by the vivid detail of color, taste and sound.

The resonating echoes of Jet are new to me. When Jet blacked out in the art room I felt a change. As if I was transported I saw her arguing with her parents over a dance her father had forbidden her to attend. Hardly something to lose sleep over but I've learned over the years that mortals take little things and roll them into big things. The tiniest of insects can topple the tallest of trees, especially when the little bugs are great in number. En masse, the littlest bugs can become insurmountable. Jet found her little worries an agonizingly heavy cross to bear and so she did something drastic about it. If only she had waited until this bad moment in her life had passed.

And what of my beloved Ben? Watching him slip in and out of consciousness as he struggles to recall his past is pain like nothing I have ever felt. Yet last night a miracle happened. Ben finally recalled a memory of a house raid. The platoons often did house raids, ransacking the homes, looking for weapons and terrorists. The more obvious it became that there were no weapons the more they kicked the stuffing out of the houses. And they took every male over five feet tall, tied their hands, and loaded them onto a truck that would take them to detention centers. This included boys.

Ben always puked whenever his sergeant ordered a house raid in retaliation for a mortar attack. Ben went along because he was ordered to. I stood by and did nothing for the same reason. I am ordered to do nothing but watch over the mortals.

Heaven help me for saying this, but I should have acted. Even the meek shepherd who tends over a flock of sheep will kill the occasional wolf.

Chapter Eighteen

The living room was warm and bright though not with the cheer of a summer's day. Not the kind of day where blowflies buzzed and birds chirped. No children squealing in the background. No dogs barking. No clanking sounds of dishes being washed or the whir of carpets being vacuumed. Just warm and bright. Quiet. Still. Phony, even. Had it always been this way, Rachael wondered? The only realness she could recall encountering was the evil presence in the art room.

She couldn't remember much about her experience in the art room, except that she'd clutched at a paintbrush, overcome with a compulsive need to paint dead eyes, until Ben and Jet had rescued her. Her head had been thick with a fog or mist or whatever that white stuff was that floated around the room. Nor could she remember Jet's promise that she would participate in Group. But when Jet had summoned them, Rachael knew she was not going to miss this for anything.

With Neale, the Group numbered four. Two mortals. Two angels. Each one with secrets. Jet was about to reveal hers, and Rachael's chest swelled with pride. She'd always known Jet would come around to her way of thinking.

Sitting in the warm, bright room, Jet appeared nervous. Rachael wanted to hug Jet but physical contact was forbidden. Instead, Rachael waited, folding her hands in her lap, the gesture she used to control them.

At last Jet cleared her throat and began to read. "My father had banned me from attending my end of year school dance. I was so mad I snuck out of the house to go to a party with Lucas. The party was everything I imagined it to be. Loud music. Tons of kids. Even though it was a warm night, a fire was going strong in a steel barrel on the back lawn. The place had a swimming pool, just an above-ground type. Kids were splashing and playing, so Lucas and I got soaked. He dragged me inside the house and I remember laughing because he was acting like such a party pooper. I mean, he invited me. What was up with him?"

Rachael glanced at Neale. His gaze was fixed on his lap, and he was squirming in his seat like he needed to go to the toilet. But angels had no use for food, drink or the need to process their waste. He was fidgeting for another reason. This wasn't a good time to ask him if he had a problem or even to elbow him to quit, and thankfully he stopped fidgeting on his own accord.

Jet continued, "I'll jump ahead to the following morning because that's when the story really starts. My head felt as if it was pushing its way outside my skull. I couldn't sit up without throwing up. Mom thought I had the flu. I didn't dare tell her I was hung over, mostly because I'd never experienced a hangover so I wasn't exactly sure what I was suffering from.

"Anyway, I thought I was going to die. Mom let me stay at home that day, but later on when I was well enough to eat a plate of leftover mashed potato she told me that exams were coming and she didn't want me to miss any more days of school."

Rachael snuck a look over in Ben's direction. Sitting on the edge of his chair, he seemed enchanted by Jet's voice.

Her insides shouldn't have swarmed with remorse but they did. If only Ben and Jet had met when they were both alive, they might both still be alive.

"So even though I was no longer puking my guts up, I felt as if I had eaten a big bowlful of rotten, curdled guilt. I was filled with dread just packing my school bag that I think I did it like twenty times. To be honest I had no idea why I was so scared. I'd had a night out and had fun. Big deal. But my mind was jammed with shame. Only in hindsight do I realize I was having a premonition. Anyway, my first class at school the next day was English. I hate English. Mostly because the girl I hate most in the world, Tanna Brown, is in my English class. She is a stuck-up bitch who hates everyone because she lived in France till her parents got divorced."

Jet paused and looked up from the book in her lap. Rachael got the impression she was going to get up and leave. Instead, Jet burst into tears.

"Tanna's made my life a living hell since the day she showed up wearing a stupid beret and talking in a poser French accent. I have no idea why she hates me. She just does."

"Sometimes chicks can be such bitches," said Ben.

Jet wiped the tears from her cheek. "Tell me about it. Maybe if another student had confronted me things might have turned out differently."

"You don't have to go on," Rachael said.

"Why don't we take a break?" Neale asked in a soft voice.

Jet shook her head. "No. I'll keep going. So there I was, walking to my English class when Tanna stopped me. She told me to follow her to the ladies' bathroom. I told her the bell was going to go off any second and if we did, we'd be late for class. She didn't care about rules, she said. The way she looked at me scared me out of my wits. If she started a fight I'd lose just because I'm not a fighter. I stood there, refusing to follow her. I would have stayed there all day except that Tanna's equally stupid friend, Britony, grabbed my school bag and ran off with it."

Rachael choked on a sob. How many times had she watched mortals get bullied and wished with all her heart for the ability to step in? But angels were forbidden to interfere. Nor could they reveal themselves to mortals. Time travel was also out of the equation though that was simple mechanics since time travel didn't exist. If it did, she would have found a way to go back in time to the day in Jet's tale. The mortal's pain was evident, and the angel was becoming engulfed in that pain.

Jet's grip on the journal tightened. "I found Britony standing outside the ladies' bathroom with such an evil look on her face. Then she chucked my school bag inside. Even though my blood was racing I went in. That's when I saw written in black marker on all the cubicle doors were the words *Jet Jones is a slut.* I just knew Tanna was the culprit. What I didn't know was why she would deface the bathroom doors.

"'Your boyfriend azked me to write it,' Tanna said, She was talking in her stupid fake French accent. God I hate her. I also didn't believe her. Lucas would never do anything horrible to me. He loved me.

"She said, 'He alzo told me you would not believe me zo I waz to mention a little game you two love birds played where you had your hands behind your back'."

Jet's voice broke. She clutched the journal. Her hands were shaking yet her eyes were glued to the book.

Is she afraid to look at us? Rachael yearned to lean over and hold Jet's hand. But that would just introduce more problems to the situation, so she tucked her feet up under her butt.

After a minute, Jet regained her composure, and used her sleeve to blot her tears. "I hate it when I cry. Just another horrible feature we girls have to live with. I'll keep going, shall I?"

Rachael silently begged her to stop.

"I ran over and slapped her. The sound echoed throughout the room. I was shocked. Tanna was shocked, too, but for only a second. Her smug look returned, and as much as I wanted to scratch that look off her face, I was putting on a brave face of my own and channeling all of my energy into willing the ground to open up and swallow me. And you know what that bitch said? She said, 'Lucaz iz my boyfriend now.'

"Of course now that I look back on it I wish I'd told her he'd do to her what he was doing to me so good luck to her. But at the time I was crushed. So I pushed past her to get the hell away from the bathrooms, but by this stage everyone in my class was gathered around the doorway and peeking in to get a good look. They were all snickering, too, but that wasn't the worst of it. The worst was yet to come. Seconds later I received a text message. 'Jet goes like a rocket.' The message was from Lucas."

Rachael heard a groan beside her. She didn't dare look at Neale for fear of embarrassing him. He came across as inhuman, but deep down she suspected he cared as much as she did.

Jet said, "As if suffering humiliation from your boyfriend wasn't bad enough, things got worse when I started to hear a lot of other cell phones beeping. When I saw the way everyone was pointing at me I could tell they'd just gotten the same message as me. Naturally, I ran home. My mother yelled at me and practically threw me out the front door. She demanded I get back on the bus so I told her if she wanted me to go back to school she'd have to drive me herself."

Jet paused. Rachael took this moment to adjust her feet on the sofa and let out the breath she'd been holding. She noticed Neale and Ben were doing likewise.

After a minute Jet said, "Mom doesn't drive. She says she never learned but I know it's how Dad controls her. Anyway, she was terrified of Dad finding out she'd let me miss a day of school. Right then I realized I no longer cared about protecting her."

She returned her attention to her journal.

"No way was I going back to that school. So while Mom rang up the bus company to find out when the next bus was due I raced into the kitchen. In the cupboard under the sink was a bottle of floor cleaner. I took it up to my room and swallowed a couple of mouthfuls. Mom came in and saw me puking my guts up. I was allowed to stay home another day."

Bile flooded Rachael's mouth. She yearned to not only embrace Jet, but to smother her with protective wings. She did nothing. Her head fell to her chest. The shame of her inability to help a mortal kept the angel motionless.

Jet's diary closed with a thud. "That's it so far. I'll write some more later."

"Jesus." Ben groaned. "Jesus. I'm really sorry about what I said before—"

"Hey, quit torturing yourself. You didn't know. And I kept it pretty quiet about why I was here. Now you know."

When Rachael looked up, Jet was getting to her feet and wearing a grin. She lifted her head high and said, "My name is Jet Jones and I'm as cracked as the rest of you."

Neale and Ben laughed, nervously at first. Rachael joined in for Jet's sake. Then Jet motioned for all of them to stand.

Ben was first to take her cue. As he stood, he cleared his throat. "Hello. My name is...oh, crap I can't remember."

First giggles, then huge, hysterical laughter came from the group. Jet pointed at Rachael, and then lifted her finger, ordering her to stand.

Rachael found it hard to obey; disgrace kept her huddled in the sofa. Earlier, she had been flushed with pride at Jet's willingness to confess. Through confession comes healing and she'd felt responsible for Jet's progress. But what had she done instead? She'd allowed to girl to tear off the bandage off a half-healed wound. Jet had suffered, was still suffering, and in all likelihood was going to do so for a lot longer.

Ben may not have recalled how long he'd been attending these Group sessions, but Rachael did.

Ten years.

She stood. "Hi, my name is Rachael. I act as if I have all the answers written in my little book, but I have no idea what I'm doing. Please don't tell anyone or they won't let me practice on you anymore."

More screams of laughter. When they died, all eyes— including Rachael's—turned to Neale, the only one left sitting on the sofa.

He held up his hands. "Not me. I'm the observer."

"You're the most nonobserving observer I've ever met." Jet scoffed.

Neale looked off into the distance as a tender smile played on his lips. His nose crinkled as though he was wracking his brain for something to say.

He faced the group one by one and an expression of concealed amusement brightened his usual calm expression.

"The name's Neale. I'm a vegetarian, eco/pet/gay friendly Sagittarius who is a bit of know-it-all and for this reason I'm banned from ever getting a library card."

His speech had them all in stitches. Only Rachael saw the look of worry on his face. This was no laughing matter. He'd said it twice and still the implication had not sunk in.

Time was not simply running out, it had long gone.

Chapter Nineteen

Kids are running toward me. '"Don't run,"' I yell. But something is coming after them. I start to run too, because I can see who is chasing them. My God it's me…

A small girl is carrying a huge bag. The bag is a dark fabric and it's ten times bigger than she is. Walking along the middle of the road, I can see she's heading straight for us. But you can't trust anyone out here. Not even kids. Still, she must be all of ten. Someone throws a grenade. When the dust settles a few apples roll toward us. One stops at my feet. She was bringing us food. And we blew her to pieces for it.

* * *

Ben's eyes flew open. He must have fallen asleep on the sofa again. A scream was trapped in his throat but he managed to choke it down.

"Where am I?"

"You had a bad dream." Rachael's voice croaked as if she was the one who'd awakened from the nightmare.

"Is there any other kind?"

Jet appeared at his side, clutching his arm, concern written all over her face. "Do you want to talk about it?"

The sympathy shining from her blue eyes should have softened his anger. Instead, it fueled it. Why did she have to care so much about him? He deserved revulsion, not compassion.

"Leave me the hell alone," he shouted, rocketing out of the chair and pushing past her. Jet called out after him but he was already out the door and running down the corridor. Running as though his life was under threat by enemy fire, running the way he'd seen the young girl in his dreams run. He could have run forever but he was stopped by a bridge that crossed over a lake.

Since when did his home town of Riggins have a bridge like this one?

Halfway up the overpass the world appeared to be covered in a thick blanket of fog. Something sinister dwelled in the fog, chilling his insides.

Neale came up beside him with all the stealth of an elephant. "If you want to talk about your dreams, I'm also a good listener."

Ben chuckled, his anger already waning, but he wanted to hold onto his anger because without it, he had nothing inside.

"You don't get the point of observing, do you?" Ben said.

Neale's grin was lopsided. "I'm sort of obligated to be here. Might as well make myself useful."

"You sound like Rachael. Always acting like she operates a confessional box." He paused and kicked the ground. "I haven't spent much time in church lately. I used to go a lot when my dad was alive."

"What happened to him?"

"Cancer."

Ben's mind shifted gears once more and he was teetering on the edge of a cliff…

How had he gotten there? Nothing stirred in the sea below, despite the hundreds of whitecaps on the surface. No breeze to push the waves into whitecaps. All was still. The whitecaps looked like blobs of white paint dabbed onto a giant canvas.

Nothing stirred on the air around him. The cries of seagulls should have danced on the breeze. Coils of air should have tickled his near naked head. He should be swatting at insects. The midday sun should have caused perspiration or thirst. He experienced none of these things. All around was an eerie nothingness. Only the shiver in his bones proved he was alive.

Had time frozen?

He sniffed as though picking up an evil scent.

"This is wrong."

Beside him, Neale remained silent. He seemed to be staring at the horizon, and Ben wondered if he felt the same as he did, like they were standing inside a giant painting...

Suddenly the chill disappeared and Ben was trapped beneath an eternal sunset choked with orange dust. The air was hot and muggy. His clothes clung to his frail body. How had he lost so much weight? Missing from the sky were the flares that shot upwards, causing the false daylight that messed with the body's natural sleeping clock. Missing, too, was the loud rock music intended to torture the enemy with sleep deprivation but also affected the allied troops.

Wake up, Ben. You know this isn't real.

The heat disappeared. He stood at the foot of the unfamiliar bridge.

"I always tried to make Dad proud of me," Ben said. "But I must have done something really bad, even if I can't remember it. I wish I'd died in the war so I wouldn't have to struggle every day to remember the bits and pieces."

He closed his eyes and waited for a soft breeze to kiss his cheek. But the air remained unnaturally still.

There is something very wrong with this place.

"The truth is within you." Neale spoke as if he'd read his mind.

Ben nodded. Neale was right of course. The truth was within. But Ben was afraid to go looking.

"My dad once said that truth had teeth sharper than any animal or knife. It cut deeper and bled longer and could cause a man considerable pain if he didn't know how to treat it properly."

Neal's voice drifted to him as if floating on the breeze. "Did he ever tell you how to treat a cut from truth?"

"He said only God could do that. Guess I'm in trouble. No God can help me escape my living hell."

Chapter Twenty

Jet breathed deeply, preparing herself for another session of Group. The one yesterday had left her emotionally wrecked. This was the point when the cleansing was meant to start, yet she felt no different.

Still, she had started something so she might as well finish it. "Right, where did I get up to?"

And just as quickly as her confidence rose within her chest, it fled back toward her feet and she wondered if she should bother going on at all. Maybe the others were just humoring her. Maybe Rachael had lied when she'd said Group wasn't compulsory.

When Jet looked up she saw every face awash with kindness. This shared empathy was what she needed to spur her on. She opened her journal, and her voice held firm as she read:

"I got a total of sixty text messages over the next few days. All of them were horrible. Jet puts out, just get her drunk. Jet goes like a rocket. Slut. Whore."

Shame at her stupidity overwhelmed her. Heat flushed her cheeks, and she looked away. "I can't believe I read every message, but I was hoping that one of my friends would send me something supportive."

Avoiding eye contact, she continued:

"So there I was with my head over the bowl puking up my guts from floor cleaner, after poisoning and torturing myself by reading all the insults people didn't have the guts to say to my face. When I stumbled back into my room Mom was sitting on my bed. From the way her back was stiff and straight, and from the blistering look on her face, I knew she'd read through my messages.

"Mom asked me if what the messages said was true. I was so angry. Why would she ask me that? I was her daughter. Surely the better question was whether I was okay.

"I told her, 'Of course it's not true. Do I look like a rocket?'"

She hesitated and looked at the others through wet lashes. She would have been fine if they wanted to laugh at her attempts to make light of her tragedy, but she was secretly glad that no one did.

"Anyway, Mom's face went red, whether with anger or embarrassment, probably both. She said, 'I don't mean about what these say' and then she threw the phone against the wall. She was pissed. Me, too. It'd taken me forever to get that phone. She then asked me, 'Is it true you had sex with that boy?'

"To be honest, I wasn't exactly sure what happened that night. All I remember was I'd gone out to the party and because I was so angry at my parents I spent the night tossing back drinks like I was drowning and they were saving my life. Stupid analogy really, the last thing you give a drowning person is more liquids.

"But I digress. That night, Lucas and I were dancing, and because I was getting drunk I started dancing provocatively. Lucas shouted in my ear that he had something he wanted to tell me. The music was blaring so loudly that we had to move into a corner to talk. I had a feeling he was going to tell me he loved me. I wanted to make sure I could hear him clearly so I led him upstairs to one of the bedrooms where we could be alone."

Chapter Twenty-One

Rachael had spent her existence separated from humans, watching their lives as though she were enjoying a trip to the zoo or looking through the glass into a police interrogation room. As she listened to Jet's tale, Rachael was still trapped inside that bubble, imprisoned inside a glass cage.

As Jet talked, she blinked and rubbed her hands across her eyes to ward off tears. Rachael wanted to bash her fists against the window, get to Jet, and comfort her. Rachael didn't care if shattered glass would pierce her hands. She was sick of living in a bubble.

But wasn't she meant to be watching Ben? Ben, who was captivated by Jet, staring at her with the love and intensity of a mother gazing at her newborn. How would Jet feel when he ascended to Heaven, leaving her alone?

But when Ben ascended, Jet wouldn't be the only person left behind.

What would become of her?

She was struck by a terrifying thought.

Have I kept him trapped here?

Deep down Rachael had always known that once Ben was well enough to leave her, he would. She would be alone. And once he was gone, what sort of existence would she have?

Her mouth went dry as her mind raced. Obviously she would get a new assignment. Angels were created for work.

But could she stay hidden in the shadows after experiencing the bliss of human interaction? These past ten years in Ben's company had fulfilled her more than had the previous three centuries.

The room began spinning, and she hauled herself upright in her seat, forcing her mind to stay focused. But the bright light streaming in from the window made her groggy.

"I'm not boring you, am I Rach?" asked Jet with a smile.

"You could never bore me."

Jet blew her a kiss. "All right. Where was I?"

In a quiet, yet steady voice Jet read:

"Lucas grabbed another bottle of liquor. I couldn't read the label. My vision was all fuzzy and frankly I couldn't have cared less if he'd swiped the cooking sherry. He took the bottle upstairs and I remember we started playing a game. He went first. He held his hands behind his back while I French kissed him. The 'no touching' with anything other than the lips is meant to heighten the kiss. When my turn came to hold my hands behind my back, Lucas put his hands up my top. I can't remember what happened next because the room started spinning.

"When I woke up I was alone. I was half-undressed and terrified because I didn't know where I was. I grabbed my jeans and climbed out the window. Embarrassed, I couldn't bear anyone seeing me walking down the stairs. I remember now how stupid I was for slipping into my jeans while up on the roof. I could have fallen to my death.

"Anyway, I made it home just as the sun was rising. Sneaking back in wasn't as easy as sneaking out but I did it somehow."

Jet slammed her journal shut. She closed her eyes and let her head fall back into the armchair as she continued with her painful story, except she was reciting it from memory.

"Mom wanted to call the police but I had no proof that anything happened. I still have none. Besides, I just wanted to forget all about it, put it down to a bad experience. You know like, hey you're a big girl now, welcome to adulthood. Mom was adamant that we had to tell Dad."

Jet let out a solitary breath and it seemed to plunge the room into an ethereal silence, quiet as a forest dawn.

Neale spoke first. "You must have been frightened and lonely."

Jet stood and walked to the window. She stared out across the ocean, yet her mind was clearly on the past. She wrapped her arms around her waist.

"I've never felt so alone in my whole life. What happened was bad enough, but keeping it a secret was even harder. I found myself walking each night to the blowhole near our home. At night I would cling to the ropes and stare into the dark water, wishing to fall. I hated my life. Hated myself. Mom wouldn't make eye contact with me. Dad was gifted with a suspicious mind so he guessed something was up. He kept demanding to know what secret I was hiding. In the end I told him I was stressing out about the exams."

When Jet turned back to face them, a look of surprise flittered across her features, as though she had forgotten they were in the room with her. Perhaps, in her mind, she was back on that cliff edge, hoping to fall into oblivion.

She shook her head. "Mom decided she wouldn't keep it a secret anymore. I told her that if she said anything I'd tell Dad she was having an affair. Whether it was true or not didn't matter. He'd have believed it because he wanted to. So she compromised by deciding to tell him in private while they were out a friend's house because Dad was such a poser he wouldn't *dare* explode in public."

She laughed and it sounded harsh and cruel. Rachael

longed to embrace her, to take her pain away.

Rachael had always wanted to know what human pain felt like, and now she was sick to the stomach at the prospect of losing her beloved Ben. Mortals were stronger than she'd realized. Perhaps she had it wrong. Perhaps angels needed mortal more.

Nobody uttered a word as Jet returned to sit with them on the sofa, yet Rachael could tell Jet's story was not finished.

"That night, while they were out discussing whether I was spending eternity in a tower or a coffin, I called Lucas. I had to know why he'd do something so horrible to me, only a few hours after telling me how much he loved me."

Rachael's stomach tightened as she braced for the wicked truth. She'd sensed something about the girl when Jet had arrived, but hadn't identified it correctly. Jet hadn't brought trouble. She'd brought baggage. And if Rachael had failed to detect Jet's baggage, had she also failed to detect the reason Ben was here?

"You know what he told me?" Jet spoke softly yet it had the strength to snatch Rachael's wandering mind and haul it back into the room. "He loved me but he wasn't *in* love with me. He wanted to break up in a way that I wouldn't beg him to take me back. He had the nerve to say he despised clingy girls."

Jet turned her journal over in her hands. She gave it a curious look, as though she had never seen it before, then stood and walked purposefully over to the bin.

She held her book over the opening. "I don't need this anymore." She let go of her journal and watched as it fell into the bin. The loud clunk heralded finality. "It ends with me trying to kill myself by drinking a bottle of vodka and swallowing a bottle of sleeping pills."

Chapter Twenty-Two

I hear the wind whisper, "I have a bad feeling about this". I have to agree but it's too late to change my mind. Seeking comfort, I reach into my shirt for the cross on the necklace. It once belonged to my dad. The wind also tells me I should be at home with my mom and my kid sister. But I am there. In spirit.

What a cop-out of an excuse. When has a spirit ever been a stand-in for the real thing?

My heart begins beating a million miles a minute. Liar, my inner voice whispers, echoing my earlier thoughts. How can you protect them from the other side of the world?

"Relax. Everything will be all right," I say out loud.

Provided I make it across the desert without dying first. Sure it looks abandoned and barren of all life, yet we've been dodging gun and mortar fire since we crossed the border. Although, for the life of me I can't understand why anyone would want to defend this shithole of a place. Not even a freaking tree grows here.

"I'm here to keep my homeland safe," I say, more as a way of keeping myself comforted. Nothing I do can bring enough inner peace to stop my heart from pounding within my chest. Forget about a grenade going off, I'm likely to explode.

A round of cheers erupts from the back of the truck, and I'm left chilled to the bone that I'm supposed to rely on these idiots to keep me safe?

I keep my eyes on my feet as the convoy of flatbed trucks, carrying hundreds of troops, weapons, Abrams tanks, armored *personnel carriers and Humvees, chugs its way to the compound that is to be our base for the six months. I should've known at boot camp that I was making a big mistake, trading a loving home for this.*

The convoy passes a burned-out tank on the side of the road. Everyone is quiet and staring at the ruins, checking to see whether it's one of our trucks or the enemy's. I suspect it's one of ours even before the look on the face of everyone around me hints that they do, too.

Someone a few rows behind yells out, "Oh yeah, you're gonna get it now you freakin' sons of bitches," and an echo of cheers follows. Outside, the sand swirls like something invisible has picked up in anger. Pretty soon the ground and sky are painted flame orange. All around me, soldiers pull their goggles down to cover their eyes. But the Perspex does nothing to stop the place looking like a Christmas tree from hell.

* * *

Ben woke up. Darkness filled the room and save for the pale shadows that clung to the cornices like spider webs he would have thought he was blind. He reached for his journal, kept under his pillow. It was hard to find a blank page in the dark, but he didn't care if he wrote over another entry. For all he cared, his book could end up a mess of dark ink, much like his scrambled brain.

He grinned at the notion, then added his dream to his collection. He finished by writing: *I wake up covered in sweat and with a scream trapped in my throat. One day I will wake up and the scream will find its way out. When that happens I doubt*

I'll be able to stop.

His head was still muddled from the nightmare so he added another bleak thought:

I used to dream of girls and cars, now I dream of decapitated heads and dead children.

As soon as he put his head back on the pillow the little bug in his head started sniggering. Crap. No point trying to get any sleep. He again opened his journal and wrote every bleak and honest thought that came to him until his eyes began to fall.

The little bug in his head waddled up to the spot behind his eyes and waved at him.

Hey. Remember when you enlisted in the army and came home wearing a combat uniform and your hair was shaved off? Mom got so upset she ran out of the house screaming.

No, that wasn't right, he told the little bug. She had run off screaming because she hadn't recognized her son, and it wasn't the only time.

The first time that had happened, he'd walked into the house after going to the movies with friends. Witchlike, she'd flown at him with a broomstick in one hand and a fry pan in the other. As she belted him over the head she screamed *Rape! Rape!* Luckily, his sister had woken up and saved him.

Another time he'd sneaked in through a window because he'd forgotten his keys. His mom had confronted him with a rifle. He was alive only because she was a terrible shot. Her memory may have faded but not her survival instinct.

Another time, Mom had changed the door lock without telling anybody so his key hadn't worked. While he was fiddling with his key in the lock she called the cops.

By this stage the police and practically the whole town had guessed that something was wrong with his mother.

Admitting to himself that his mom was losing her mind was the toughest truth he had ever swallowed. Nobody asked how she was doing anymore. Nobody struck up any sort of conversation with Crazy Mrs. Taylor for fear of hearing what nobody wanted to hear, that craziness wasn't choosy about who it tagged.

Watching her had broken his heart. She'd sit at the dining table with her crossword pages in front of her, crying her eyes out because she couldn't remember the four-letter word for 'something you cook in'. He'd fooled his mind into believing she would be all right. Despite his conviction, her condition worsened.

After his dad died, life had changed for Ben and his younger sister. When his mother fell ill, life had changed insurmountably more. His world had gotten so intolerable he'd joined the army to free himself of the burden of responsibility.

He acted as if distance could blot out his mother's illness. Abandonment, desertion, disregard, neglect, running away had changed nothing. He had pushed his mother's illness into the deepest chamber of his mind.

Everything buried becomes unearthed eventually. And it didn't take the nagging voice in his head to remind him of this.

Chapter Twenty-Three

Jet woke with a start. Shouts were coming from the boys' room. She immediately presumed one of them was having a nightmare, and she'd put a hundred bucks on which one of them she'd find tangled in the sheets.

Her instincts proved correct. She opened the door to see Ben tossing around on his bed, his legs and arms spasmodically kicking and twisting in the sheets.

"I couldn't do it," he cried out. "Sergeant told me to, but I couldn't do it."

Neale sat on the opposite bed. Where Ben had a face emblazoned with physical pain, Neale wore an expression of serenity. "Of course you couldn't," Neale said. "You're not an evil person."

"All she wanted was food. 'Mister food. Mister food.' She kept coming back. What harm was there in giving her food? We had more than enough."

"Was she a terrorist?" Neale reached out a hand but it hovered over Ben's brow, as though afraid to make contact. "Was she the enemy?"

"God, no," Ben groaned.

Jet opened the door wider. A blast of cold air assaulted her, yet Ben was covered in sweat. "Hey. Is he all right?"

She got no answer from either Ben or Neale. They appeared to be deep in conversation, so she decided to leave. Then Neale beckoned her into the room. He patted the bed next to where he sat and put his finger to his lips.

"She was a kid. I did nothing to stop her getting killed." Ben was screaming. His eyes were scooting around inside his head faster than pinballs. "She kept coming back to visit me. I once got a fox to return to the campsite by feeding it. I got the girl killed just like I got that fox killed."

He suddenly sprang into an upright position.

Jet started to bolt but his hand shot out and grabbed her by the wrist.

"Get away from me! Run! I am evil!"

She sat trembling and forcing whimpers down into her chest for his sake. His gaze latched onto hers though it seemed to pass through her at the same time.

Rachael appeared at the doorway, bringing with her the calming influence she was noted for so Jet was spared the scream she felt erupting from within.

"What's going on?" Rachael asked.

Neale stood up. "His time is almost here."

Jet managed to pull her wrist free but her heart was still beating a million miles an hour. "Time for what? Are they going to take him away? Please don't let them do it. It wasn't his fault that he—"

"Yes!" Ben's wild eyes searched and found her. "It was my fault. I should never have abandoned her."

Ben tried to untangle himself from the bedsheets without success.

Jet gaped at Ben. She was remembering to the time he'd strangled her but she realized he was talking about something else entirely.

How many secrets does this guy have?

"His memory is coming back to him," Neale told her. "Soon he will unlock the memory that has kept him here."

Like in *The Exorcist*, Ben twisted and turned on the bed.

Pillows flew about the room. He knocked over the bedside lamp yet instead of plunging the room into darkness, an iridescent glow washed the walls, as though the moon was streaming in through the cracks. But there were no cracks. The windows in the room were covered with heavy curtains.

Jet was about to ask if the others noticed the eerie light when Ben collapsed onto the floor, his body limp. Before she could rush over to see if he was dead he sat up and smiled. With an air of calm he stretched and yawned, then stood up and reached for his shirt.

He put it on and left the room with the other three following. He went to the bathroom and stopped in front of the mirror. "I should never have left you, Mother. What a weak thing to do. Cowardly."

Ben turned to face Jet, and she was struck frozen.

"She needed me," he said. "They both did. I left my kid sister to care for my mom while I went off to war. I should have stayed to look after them. I am the man of the house."

"What's wrong with your mother?" Jet asked, her voice clogged with fear.

Ben buttoned up his shirtsleeves and went to the living room, where he began punching the cushions till they were fat and fluffy. "Everything has to be just how she remembers it. Otherwise she'll freak out and accuse us of playing tricks on her. Do you know how hard it is to constantly run around after someone who forgets everything?"

Jet bit her tongue. Now was not the time to point out the irony.

"I've lost count of the number of times Mom nearly burned the house down from leaving the stove on." He paused and stared at Rachael. "You remember how many times the fire department came to the house?"

"I'm not your sister," Rachael squeaked.

Ben stared at her. His eyes flicked rapidly the way a reptile blinks.

"You could be though. You have her red hair and green eyes."

He must be hallucinating, Jet thought. Rachael had black hair and blue eyes, just like her.

Ben patted the top of the sofa. "All right. Everything is back where it belongs. Where's Mom?"

Empathy for Ben washed through her and her insides tightened. He'd often spoken of his mother with obvious love, but she was struck with the horrifying thought that his mother was dead and he had no idea. Poor guy.

Without warning, he marched to the kitchen, which was to the left of the open-plan living room, and stopped in front of the fridge. "She usually leaves a note."

His eyes scoured the fridge. Its exterior was spotless. Not even a brand name marred its surface.

"Ah, found one. She's at work." Ben shook his head. "She hasn't worked at the motel for years. The manager will be calling soon to demand I collect her."

This was scarier than the first time Ben had read from his journal;

"Stop cracking up," Jet cried out. "Ben, they'll take you away and we'll be separated." She became hysterical. "Somebody get a doctor. Please. Where are the doctors? Tell them you're making this up. Tell them you're okay. Why is everyone standing around doing nothing? Somebody get a doctor!"

A flicker of alertness crossed Ben's gaze, and he visibly paled. Then like a candle in a storm the light in his eyes went out.

"Doctors? Mom doesn't like strangers in the house. She thinks everyone is trying to steal the TV."

Where does he think he is?

She grabbed his shoulders and shook him, hard. Her blood chilled but she had to ask anyway. "Ben, tell me what you see."

He gave her a mischievous grin. "I see a beautiful angel come to save me."

Flattery was wasted while she in her current mood. "Get a grip. I might be angelic, but I'm no angel."

"You will always be an angel to me."

"Stop fooling around. Where are you? What do you see?" Her lips trembled as she braced herself for his answer. She would have bet her life they each saw the living room differently. She would also have bet he hadn't noticed the pool on the rooftop or the colorful painting of a turtle or the shell-covered vase. If he gazed out the glass doors that led to the balcony, would he look down at the path that wound through palm trees to the ocean?

"What do you see?" she asked.

"My home." His brows drew together and anxious eyes searched hers.

He was telling the truth. She breathed out slowly. He really was seeing another place altogether. No wonder they'd given each other strange looks. No wonder he was dead set on fixing the sink that wasn't broken.

"Describe it to me."

He gave her another weirded-out look but pointed to a spot on his right. "Mom got that dining table from the church rummage sale. Over there is our toy box. I painted it red like a fire truck. Next to it is the faded leather armchair she sits in to do her crosswords. You can't even tell its leather anymore, 'cos she covers it with blankets." His face contorted slightly. "Something's missing though. The walls are supposed to be filled with photos. I can't see any photos."

This explained something, but she didn't know what. The room Ben described was very different to the one Jet saw. She guessed he saw his home, in Riggins, Idaho. She believed she was on Magnetic Island in Queensland, Australia. The room she was in looked exactly like the one portrayed in the brochure she'd found hidden in her father's car.

Her eyes widened. Had she mentally projected this image?

"What about the mirror?" she said. At least they both saw that.

Ben lifted his arm up to shield his face. "Who turned up the light? It hurts my eyes."

Neale stepped in and took his arm. "Time to go, buddy."

"Where are you taking him?" Jet grabbed Ben by the arm and was determined to hang on. Neale stared at her hand but she glared back; she wasn't going to let him intimidate her.

But then her fingers began to hurt as though an invisible force was tearing them off Ben.

Ben had told her something invisible had pulled his hands off her throat. Again, he'd told the truth.

As her hand dropped away she smelled the ocean, though not the pleasant scent of waves. This aroma was the stench of rotting sea animals.

Neale stared into her eyes and she knew who had saved her.

"When Ben was strangling me, you were the one who saved me," she whispered. "Why would you do that?"

Neale didn't answer. Instead, he guided Ben to the full-length mirror. When Neale reached out a hand, his white fingertips passed through the glass.

"Where are you taking him?" Jet cried.

"Where he belongs."

The two men stepped up to the mirror but Ben held back. He turned to face Jet.

She ran to him and grabbed his hands, lifting them to her cheeks. "Stay here with me. We'll do whatever you want. Hiking. Camping. Swimming."

"I saw a lake. It had a paddle wheeler and black swans. The little bug in my head told me it wasn't real."

She squeezed her eyes to stop the flow of tears but they fell anyway. "We'll go for a paddle. Whatever you want, just stay with me. I'm sorry I said I hated you. I don't, you know. I love you."

Her face was warm and Ben's hands were cool and wet with her tears. He didn't pull away, but his thumbs drew gentle circles on her cheeks. Their gazes locked, and she was certain he loved her, too.

"If you love me, then I truly am saved." He turned his head toward Rachael. "Can you get me my journal please? It's in my room under my pillow."

Rachael left, returning with his diary. She held it out, an arm's length away from Ben. Annoyed with Rachael's phobia over physical contact, Jet grabbed the journal and gave it to Ben.

He flicked through the pages, tore out one near the end, and handed it to Jet. "Promise me you'll give this to my mom. I let her down when I ran away. I know now I'll never get the chance to tell her how truly sorry I am."

Jet wanted to tell him to give it to her himself, the way they did in the movies, but all she managed was a weak nod of her head.

"I loved you from the moment I saw you," Ben told her. "It sounds trite, but I did."

"It's not trite. It's perfect."

Jet threw herself at him and her lips sought his. This time he didn't try to strangle her. Finally, she experience the perfect fairy tale kiss, and her stomach dropped when she realized she would feel dead inside for all eternity because she'd never again see him, touch him, kiss him.

Their lips were locked, and she wanted to stay connected to him, but Ben pulled away. He touched her cheek and whispered, "I'll never forget you."

"We'll see each other again. Promise."

But Ben and Neale stepped through the mirror and disappeared.

As its reflective surface frosted, her brain began scrambling to convince itself that everyone was playing a cruel trick on her and that in the next second, every cell phone on the planet would chime and the whole world would know a boy had made a fool of her again.

Only this time she would have gladly suffered the humiliation rather than accept that Ben was gone and could never return.

Chapter Twenty-Four

Jet turned away from the mirror to find Rachael seated on the sofa, looking dazed.

"What are you upset about?" Jet demanded.

"He finally crossed over."

"What are you talking about? Crossed over to where?"

"Heaven." Rachael spoke as if Heaven was the café on the corner, not some fictional place.

Jet snorted out loud. "Heaven doesn't exist."

"Of course it does. That mirror is the doorway."

Jet shook her head. "This has to be a stupid hoax. Who are you? And who set you up to trick me? Was it Lucas?"

"This is no trick."

"I saw you in the mirror." Jet pointed her finger at Rachael, glad to have someone on whom she could vent her rage and loss. "You had wings. You and Neale. You both had wings. This has to be an illusion."

Rachael straightened her back, sitting primly on the sofa, hands folded. "Calm down. You are right that I have wings. That's because I am a guardian angel—"

"Do you think I'm an idiot?"

"—and as an angel I am forbidden to reveal my true self or purpose to a mortal—"

"You do think I'm an idiot."

"—when the mirror lit up to take Ben away you were able to see Neale and me for what we really are. Before that we had to wear what we call a glimmer so you'd see us how you wanted to."

Jet gritted her teeth till they hurt. "So everyone is in on this practical joke?"

"Please listen to me. This is not a joke. Until a moment ago I was Ben Taylor's guardian angel. He saw me as his kid sister. I think you saw you me as a kid sister, too. One you never had but always wanted. Why is that?"

Jet wanted to stab her finger into Rachael's eye. "Stop using your psychobabble on me." Hysteria bubbled and she flapped her arms about. "Oh my God, this isn't happening."

"Please calm down. Let me explain how Ben died and we both ended up in Purgatory, where we've been trapped ever since. What I can't explain is your presence."

Jet flung her panic aside and dried her eyes by running her bare arm across her face.

"I drank a bottle of vodka and swallowed a bottle of pills. Where else am I gonna end up?"

Rachael stared at her curiously, chewing on her lower lip. "You seem to be taking this very well. Better than I'd have expected."

Jet shrugged her shoulders and turned to face the mirror.

"Yeah, well, I guessed something was wrong the minute I got here. This place is too good to be true. Which means it isn't. Nothing that's happening is normal. I'm never hungry. A doctor hasn't come to check up on us. My parents didn't even come to visit me. Maybe my dad would ditch me, but not my mom. She would have come."

"I still say you're taking this well. I had you figured for a drama queen."

Jet's face flushed as a renewed wave of fury swamped her.

"Taking it well? Hardly. I'm doing what I always do by

pretending everything is fine. It's what the women in the Jones house do. Believe me, I'm going ballistic on the inside. Yes, I wanted to go to a tropical resort, just not in freaking Purgatory." Then she started taking huge gulps of air, madly flailing her arms and shrieking how she was in freaking Purgatory.

"Stop that," Rachel scolded. "You'll hurt yourself!"

"How can I hurt myself when I'm dead?" Jet yelled. "Did you hear me? I'm dead. Do you have any idea what that feels like? Of course not. Well, I shouldn't know what it feels like either." She burst into tears and hid her face with her hands. Everything inside shook and ached as her bottomless well of tears sought to empty.

"Do you want that hug now?" Rachael asked softly.

Jet lifted her head and nodded. A moment later, the soft tickle of feathers engulfed her. Everything around her brightened. The light surrounding her contained sound, a melodic vibration that hummed along the angel's feathers.

Odd but soothingly hypnotic.

Her senses began to switch off, and her pain receded, as though Rachael's wings contained a trance-inducing drug.

"I promise to get you out of here as fast as I can." Rachael's voice sounded far away. Worse, it sounded unconvincing.

Something awoke in Jet, a niggling suspicion that the angel's wings didn't signify safety the way they ought. More likely they were a smothering trap, one in which she didn't want to stay. So she hauled herself to sit upright and the angel's winged parted, spanning the breadth of the room.

Awe swept over Jet at the sight and she wanted to quickly wrap herself in the wings again. But they were a false security. She held onto Rachael's comforting hand, though.

"You mean you'll help me like the way you helped Ben? I think you wanted to keep him here, and that's why he got stuck."

"Perhaps. I never had a mortal talk back to me before."

"You can't keep me against my will."

The angel sighed, a sound like trees falling in a forest. "I know. But I don't want to be alone."

"Funny, that's all I ever wanted." A shrill laugh erupted. "Oh my God, I still can't believe this is happening. I'm actually having a conversation with an angel, which means I'm dead. Very dead. Never to be resurrected. I suppose I can accept that. After all, it's what I set out to accomplish. But I never expected there would be an afterwards. I thought taking my life would be like taking a really long nap. And now I'm stuck in Purgatory reliving my shame. Why can't it be over?"

"Afterlife doesn't work that way."

"Well, it should. Otherwise, why bother dying?"

The angel sighed once more. "It usually takes death for a mortal to embrace life."

A melancholy angel. On the long list of things she hadn't expected, a doubtful angel was top of the list.

"You did a good job helping Ben," said Jet. "You never gave up on him. I'd be lucky to have you as my guardian angel."

The angel shook her head and shards of light danced around the room. "But I failed him."

"That's not true. You stayed focused on getting him to remember details about the war. You never gave up on guiding him out of his dark place. I took him for a homicidal maniac."

The angel sighed a third time, and a pang of regret stabbed Jet's stomach. As a nosy brat Rachael had driven her mental. As a Biblical figure, six feet tall, ghostly pale with wings that floated on the air and the body of a milky statue, she was more magnificent than anything Jet would ever behold. Yet she was saddened by the thought of never seeing the young girl again.

Jet squirmed away from the angel's embrace. The shift was quick. Fourteen-year-old Rachael sat on the floor looking as lost and miserable as Jet felt. This was the version of Rachael that Jet preferred, but she couldn't say why.

Jet's sweeping glance took in Rachael's long dark hair, creamy complexion, sapphire blue eyes, reasonably fashionable clothes. Why hadn't she noticed the similarity to her own features before? "You were right about me always wanting a younger sister. So you can't be all that bad at your job."

"What does it matter? I was wrong about Ben, and in my business wrong is the same as useless. I was supposed to know he wasn't repressing the war but the guilt he felt at abandoning his sick mother."

The mirror flashed, and Jet jumped.

A milky white image was dancing on the glass.

Dozens of images began dancing across the glass until the surface was white and opaque, like marble.

I can see why he was transfixed by the mirror.

If only the images would slow down so she could get a good look at them because the sense of familiarity tickled the insides of her skull.

One of the white shapes stopped, and Jet swore it smiled at her.

She gasped.

She'd seen these white shapes before.

Rachael was slumped on the floor and couldn't see the action in the mirror.

A ghostly image appeared from behind the fridge.

The room started to pulse with glowing light in tune with Jet's thoughts. She tapped Rachael on the shoulder. "Didn't you ever think it odd that Ben and I were the only, uh, people in this place? Not that I'm an expert, but Purgatory should be filled with human souls, right?"

"How should I know? It's not my job to follow you to Purgatory. Angels are only meant to shadow mortals during their lives."

"Rach, you're not listening to me. This place should be filled with *human* souls."

Rachael lifted her head and tilted it to the side like a puppy did when it heard strange noises. "I don't follow you."

Jet backed away from the mirror.

Her heart began slamming against her ribs.

White shadows were crawling across the ceiling.

"My God, it never occurred to me before, but the things in the art room and the pool. They're ghostly pale, six feet tall and they have wings."

"So?"

"So. This isn't *my* Purgatory, Rach. It's *yours*."

Chapter Twenty-Five

Angels were bound by certain rules. Rachael knew nothing of the fate that awaited an angel who broke them. Nevertheless, she pouted, lifting her chin. "That can't be right. A Purgatory for angels? Ridiculous. I would have known if there was such a thing as Purgatory for angels."

Wouldn't I, she thought?

All of a sudden she felt faint.

"Maybe you're on a need to know basis," Jet said. "You angels are messengers of God doing divine work without question. Right?"

"Yes, but we'd still know about this place."

Jet grabbed a chair from under the dining table, went to the mirror, and lifted the chair over her head.

"What are you doing?" Rachael cried out.

"You might belong here, but I don't."

"Put down that chair. Put it down immediately."

Jet lowered the chair to the floor. "Fine. What do you suggest I do to get out of here?"

Rachael gave a weary shake of her head, her mind racing as she tried to come to grips with the concept of angel limbo.

Jet began running her hands around the edge of the gold frame.

"Now what are you doing?" Rachael asked.

"What does it look like? I'm trying to find a hidden trigger lock that'll open the doorway so I can get out of here.

There's got to be a secret opening."

"Try saying Open Sesame."

"Really? That works?"

"Of course not. Heaven's Door only opens when the soul is ready to ascend. Chanting phony magical words won't help."

Jet smiled, abandoned the mirror, and ran to the bin. She retrieved the journal she'd earlier discarded and found a pen, which she scratched busily across the pages.

Rachael was intrigued. "Group is over. You don't have to write in your journal anymore."

"Are you kidding? This is my ticket out of here. You should start writing in your journal, too, unless you want to stay and paint god-awful pictures for eternity."

"What a ludicrous suggestion." Rachael laughed. "Angels don't die."

"I suppose you're also going to tell me angels are peaceful, holier-than-thou creatures whose sole purpose is to be nice to us mortals. Well, one of your righteous brethren tried to drown me in the pool. And another left a paintbrush where I tripped over it and nearly broke my neck."

"It's totally out of character for an angel to commit an act of malice. Why would we want to hurt you?"

Jet looked up from her journal. "Not hurt me. *Kill* me. And why does anyone do anything? Because they want to get noticed."

"I still say I would've heard of Purgatory for angels."

"Well, what else can this place be? Do you really think angels can turn their backs on mortals and get off without any form of retribution? Where was my guardian angel when my boyfriend got me drunk and took advantage of me?"

Rachael gasped. "Believe what you want, but the truth is

we angels never turn our backs on mortals. We do as we are told."

Blistering with rage and waving her fist above her head, Jet's teeth were clenched so tight they could have bitten through steel. "You mean my angel was told to watch and do nothing as Lucas raped me!"

Rachael cringed. She liked it better when she was the one doing the judging. "Things happen for a reason. How else do mortals learn and grow? How you deal with conflict defines who you are, not what you do to gain popularity or wealth. So many people get that bit wrong. And you said yourself, you can't be sure of what happened."

Jet stared at her open-mouthed. Then she shook her head as though changing her mind about something. Hopefully, she was changing her mind about where to direct her anger. Rachael preferred her human contact less feisty than this.

"Maybe this place is a repair shop," Jet said. "Did you ever think of that? What happens if an angel breaks a halo or a wing?"

"I don't know. I suppose you could have a point." Rachael stared at her hands. Human hands. But she was not human, and the feelings running through her were not hers.

So many mortals. So many memories. None of them mine.

"Maybe I'm here because I need fixing. There were a lot of bombs going off around Ben. A resonating shock possibly got me."

The pain of human grief she'd experienced moments ago had worn away and she found herself longing for the dull ache that crippled her legs, tightened her chest, and throbbed at her temples. She would have welcomed the pain and gladly pay the price if it meant she could connect with the mortal standing in front of her.

Angels weren't meant to experience loss or grief or

sadness. Or happiness, rage, jealousy. Or shame or failure. Or any of the other million moods humans endured. But without the sense of touch, how did one know to stay out of the fire? And without the gift of emotion, how did one develop empathy?

The angelic aloofness she'd carried with her for centuries was a hobble, not a blessing.

She covered her face and wept. The sound of rain pelting against a tin roof filled the room. "I should have known he was guilty at abandoning his mother."

Jet opened her book to the page she'd just finished and began reading:

"If the way to heaven is through forgiveness, I give it to Lucas. He was a prick and did a terrible thing but I forgive him. I should have stayed to face the consequences of my actions. And I admit I made the choice to go with him and get drunk and I chose to run away. I messed up. Please forgive me and forgive Lucas as well, so I can go to where I belong."

Jet closed her journal. "Now what happens?"

Sniffling, Rachael let her body fall across the sofa. "How should I know?"

"Rachael! What happens next?"

"You said yourself I'm here because I'm broken. As in useless, obsolete, kaput. How should I know how this place operates?"

A loud bang at the balcony door made them both jump. The glass appeared to be frosting over. A shadow-angel tugged at its handle, trying to force its way inside.

Jet grabbed her by the hand. "Get up."

Rachael promptly transformed into the six-foot tall angels, and Jet's eyes widened.

Rachael said with a smirk, "Now you know why I

couldn't let you near me. My cover would have been blown."

Jet grunted as she tried to pull Rachael toward the front door. "What about Neale's cover? He didn't morph into Big Bird when he pulled Ben through the mirror."

"Dunno. Your guess is as good as any."

Jet bit her lower lip. "Well, he seems younger than you. A newer model, maybe? A mutant? An angel more powerful than you?"

Rachael's eyes narrowed. "I don't know, okay? I don't know anything anymore. Now get out of here, will you? Leave the doomed to the damned."

Jet grabbed a feather and tugged it.

It hurt. "Ow!"

Then Jet grabbed another feather and plucked it out. She grabbed a handful and tugged.

Rachael cried, "Cut that out."

"Well, move your ass, birdie, or I swear I'll pluck you like an overgrown bikini line."

Chapter Twenty-Six

Jet was halfway to the front door when she doubled over and her insides lurched up through her throat. She threw up all over the floor.

Rachael clutched Jet and engulfed her with her wings. "What's happening? What can I do?"

Jet's throat constricted; she was unable to answer. The sensation wasn't like Ben's hands on her neck. More like fingernails scraping down the insides of her esophagus. And something was pinning her neck back till every fiber of her body ached.

Being cloaked in the angel's wings was her only comfort and she thought, *This is what it would feel like to be smothered by a cloud. Nice.*

Faces swam in front of her blurred vision, faces she couldn't name. She reached for Rachael's hand and began screaming seconds before a foreign object was wedged into her mouth.

Chapter Twenty-Seven

Rachael shrieked in agony as Jet's pain coursed through her.

Is this why angels are forbidden to touch mortals?

Their pain was unbearable.

"Take me," Rachael cried. "Do not touch the girl. I beg of you."

When a shadow appeared at the foot of the mirror, she thought her prayers were answered. The shape cast a circle of darkness in front of her. The shape turned out to be Neale. No longer wearing his glimmer, his wings spanned across the room, like the interior of an enormous pillow.

His beaming smile lit up the place. "The answer is no."

She was momentarily startled.

"What was the question?"

"Has He forsaken me?"

But He had forsaken her. If she was here, He must have. She'd messed up badly, and the only true punishment she could suffer was eternity without mortals. She couldn't survive with anything other than her angelic role. How would she cope without a mortal to watch? Might as well drop a dolphin into the desert and ask it how it planned to live.

Jet was right about one thing, though. Angels had no right to mess things up without facing the consequences.

"Give me the girl," Neale roared. "Quickly, before her

time runs out."

Rachael almost laughed. If time ran out for Jet, then mortal and angel would be trapped here together, which beat getting stuck here alone.

Chapter Twenty-Eight

Jet opened her eyes but her vision was still fuzzy. Nothing wrong with her ears, though. She could hear an awful lot of noise, and she panicked. She wasn't allowed to have people in the house.

"She's awake." A male voice. One she didn't recognize. "Julliet? I'm a paramedic. Can you hear me?"

She could but her eyes were closed and she thought, *if they can't see me, I can't get into trouble,* and she drifted back off among the clouds.

* * *

Someone was shaking her. An angel? The last thing she remembered was talking to an angel but that was absurd. Angels weren't real.

She felt her neck wobble. Someone was still shaking her. "Jet. You have to get up. Neale's here. He's come to take you away."

Jet curled herself up inside a feather blanket. Why would she leave? Where would she go? Home was a long way away, and she was perfectly fine where she was. So what if the place was a little bright? This was still the best sleep she'd ever had. Eternal slumber was the death she'd envisioned.

She was finally getting what she wanted.

Eat your heart out, Sleeping Beauty.

She pulled the feather blanket around her shoulders. "Leave me alone," she whispered.

* * *

"Leave me alone," she screamed.

"Julliet!"

Her mother was shouting at her through a thick haze. Jet was blinded. She couldn't see her mother's face. She didn't need to open her eyes to know her mother was crying.

"Julliet!" Her mother was shouting her name.

She wanted to hate her mom but something awakened inside her chest. Love. Compassion. Joy.

Then she heard another voice she recognized, and this one squeezed at her heart till it leaked cold and icy blood.

"Julliet. Come back to us, sweetheart."

Sweetheart? Since when had her father ever called her that? And why was he pretending to care about her?

He probably wants to tell me that hospitals cost money and I had better get up off the floor before I embarrass the family.

She rolled over and came face to face with a set of brown eyes.

The paramedic again.

She recognized his soothing voice.

"Stay with me, Julliet," he said. "I'm giving you something to soak up the pills and alcohol you took. It tastes horrible, but you'll be fine in a little while."

Already fine thank you, she tried to whisper but something was wedged in her throat prevented her from speaking. He was right about it tasting horrible. She tried to spit it up but choked instead.

Chapter Twenty-Nine

Rachael clung to Jet. She would not let go. Wrapping her wings around her, she began to sing an ancient lullaby. Jet was slipping in and out of the two worlds. Rachael wanted Jet to stay in this one, even though her selfishness was probably the reason she was stuck in Purgatory in the first place.

She felt Neale's presence in the room. "I know I'm supposed to hand her over but I can't let go. This is so unfair."

Neale poked her on the shoulder. "You've been hanging around mortals too long. Come on. Stop being sentimental and let go of her so I can take her back to where she belongs."

"But the shadow-angels," Rachael cried. "She needs protecting." She was terrified to admit the truth. She couldn't bear it if she was left alone. Angels were never alone. The thought of eternity as an angel in Purgatory with no mortal to watch was worse than becoming one of the threatening white shadows.

The room began to pulse with their anger. Bright webs clung to the corners, growing as if spun by invisible spiders, and began to cover the furnishings. Lights like mirror balls landed on Rachael. In response, she hugged Jet closely to her chest.

By now the shadow-angels were tugging at her wings,

trying to get her to loosen her grip. Something was screeching at her from the midst of a white storm, and it wasn't mortal. "She doesn't belong here," it hissed.

"Yeah, well who says I do?" Rachael answered.

Centuries seemed to pass while Rachael fended off her attackers. Wings thrashed, sending feathers dancing around the room like snowflakes, howls split her eardrums, sounds like nails on a blackboard sent chills down her spine. Protecting Jet was her sole purpose now. She would have died to protect her.

"Get away from her," she screamed.

Wings slapped into her back and her head. Eerie voices shrieked in her ear. Skeletal fingers tore at her feathers, hair, and clothes.

I won't let them harm her.

And then the beatings stopped and she felt her body rising into the air.

She snuck a look.

"Neale? What are you doing?"

Neale was puffing with exertion. "I told you that He has not forsaken you. I just hadn't planned on carrying you both out of here at once."

She let her head fall against his chest. "You saved me."

"You sound surprised."

"I didn't know you cared."

"Who says I care? I'm simply following orders."

Then he stepped through the mirror into darkness.

Chapter Thirty

Jet opened the car door and took a deep breath, letting the chill, pine-scented air fill her nostrils and lungs. Mountain air was something else. She could almost taste it, too.

"Will you be all right?" her mother asked. "I'll come with you if you want."

Jet smiled. Her mother had found it difficult to grasp Jet's need to fly halfway round the world to visit another mother, the mother of a dead soldier she loved madly but could only have met in her dreams. The dream was too hard to believe, and for a while Jet hadn't.

Also in her dreams there'd been a guardian angel who had saved her from dying. For a while, Jet had managed to convince herself that she'd either had a near-death experience or had hallucinated from the overdose.

Yet one morning, a few weeks after the ordeal, she'd reached into her jeans pocket and found a slip of paper that cast all doubt aside. In her pocket was the page that Ben had torn out of his journal and made her promise to give to his mom, right before he had stepped through the mirror and ascended to Heaven.

No way could she explain this to her mom. She was barely accepting it as real herself.

But how many more secrets could she burden herself with, and this time, could she handle the burden?

She hated keeping secrets but this one was easy to hold.

Besides, who would believe Purgatory existed in more than one realm, and that angels were real? Yet, knowing guardian angels were out there warmed her insides. She was glad she had proof they existed, because she needed her angel's comforting guidance more than ever.

"I'll be fine," she told her mom. "I just gotta do this."

"You do what you have to, baby. We'll be here if you need us."

Jet squeezed her mother's hand, and her mother squeezed back. When Jet tried to move her mother refused to let go.

She rolled her eyes. Her mother acted like Jet was made of tissue paper these days, or that she'd fly off with the merest hint of a breeze. She smiled. Even if she did fly away, and there was a strong chance she would – she *was* only young – she was certain that someone with a magnificent set of wings would be shadowing her.

Jet gave her mother's hand one last reassuring squeeze before she walked up the pathway to the pale gray weatherboard house. A neat row of flowers in every color possible guided her along the path that led to a tiny porch, not wide enough to hold more than one person at a time. Fat conifers edged each side of the property. Over the rooftop she counted a dozen trees, some already relieved of their foliage, others vivid with autumn. And not twenty feet away from the rear of the house a mountain rose up out of the ground, dwarfing the modest house. The mountain blocked the morning sun, but it wasn't lack of sunlight that caused a shiver along her shoulders.

Ben had lived here.

She knocked on the door and waited long enough for her to have once more rehearsed what she wanted to say, even though she'd recited the lines a million times on the long plane trip.

When the door finally opened to reveal a woman with flowing red hair and green eyes, Jet had to swallow her shock. Even though Ben's head had been closely cropped, the resemblance was still remarkable.

Yet Jet hadn't expected to see someone with a stomach so large she appeared ready to give birth at the hint of a sneeze.

"Rachael Taylor?" Jet asked.

The woman nodded.

A man appeared from around the doorway and placed his arm around her shoulder. "Only for one more week. She'll be a Gibson next Saturday. Got to make an honest woman out of her, that's if the baby can wait. Guess I should have asked her sooner, huh?" He rubbed her huge belly, his smile giving away his excitement.

Jet stared at the bulging tummy. Ben's niece or nephew was inside that ballooning stomach.

I can't do this, she thought. Panic rose in her chest.

Yes, you can, she heard the wind whisper. And the panic died down.

"Rachael," a voice called out from within the house. "Is that Ben?"

"No, Mom."

"Well, who is it?"

Alert green eyes stared at Jet, asking the same question. Despite the rehearsals in the plane, Jet bit back the tears that threatened to burst from within. This was harder than she expected.

Instinct told her to run, but she owed it to Ben to let his family know how often he'd thought of them, although how could she ever say this? What if they accused her of ridiculing them and called the police? Or worse. What if they still had some of Ben's hunting weapons and they decided not to call the police but go vigilante instead?

Rachael's green eyes softened beneath Jet's nervous stance. Ben's sister nodded in understanding and gave her future husband a kiss on the cheek. "Give me a moment, please."

He nodded and went inside the house.

Jet's palms were clammy and her throat was dry. She cleared her throat. "You don't know me, but I met your brother while he was in the...while he was recovering. We got to talking and before he...well, he asked me to give this to you."

"You met Ben? He died a while ago. Wow. You must have been a baby when you met him."

Jet shrugged her shoulders, feeling her face growing warm beneath the questioning green eyes. "Yeah, they were weird circumstances all right. Anyway, I got here as soon as I could. I promised him I'd deliver this to his mom." She thrust the page of Ben's journal under her nose.

"Mom's not up to seeing visitors." Rachael stared down at the piece of paper as if it contained toxic ink. "I'll make sure she gets it."

Jet forced the note into Rachael's hands seconds before her resolve crumbled. She burst into tears, spun on her heels and raced to the rental car. She jumped into the backseat without once glancing back.

Her father started the engine. "Where to now, sweetheart?" he asked. "Disneyland? Grand Canyon?"

She wiped a sleeve across her eyes. She should be angry at her dad but she was thrilled with his sudden change in attitude. And to think, all it took was an overdose to bring him around to loving the only daughter he had.

After Jet had woken up from her coma-like daze, her dad had explained that he'd held onto the anger of her mother seeing him and another guy at the same time. He'd also told her a something that her cousin, Steve, had failed to mention. Like how when Jet was eight months old her dad had legally adopted her. So he was in fact her father.

At the hospital he'd broken down, saying her actions had made him see just how badly he'd treated her and her mom. He'd promised to let go of the anger and become a better father. He had started proving himself immediately when Lucas had stupidly turned up at the hospital to apologize. She suspected he had come to visit only to find out if she was pressing charges. Her dad had grabbed Lucas by the collar and threatened to remove his manhood without anesthetic.

He would do whatever she wanted, Dad had said. Jet had considered giving him a long list but decided the first thing she wanted was a happy family. The second thing she wanted was for whatever secrets they'd had to stay buried. The hospital counselor told her keeping secrets was not helpful in the healing process. She'd laughed out so loud she'd coughed and spluttered. When the counselor asked her to explain what she'd found funny, she'd replied that if she could explain it, she'd get locked up in a padded room for the rest of her life.

A breeze blew in through the car window, blowing her back to the present. "Let's go to Disneyland."

If the angel, Rachael, was watching, and Jet hoped she was, a visit to the most fantastical place on the planet was probably the most suitable vacation destination.

Epilogue

Rachael of the Winter Forest clapped her hands with joy when she saw Jet walking down the path toward her.

"I'll swap assignments with you," she told Neale of the Ocean Winds. "I'll watch over Jet and you can stay here."

He gave her his famous dazzling smile. "You know we have to stick to our schedules."

"Yes, but if something bad—" she choked on the word, "—was to happen to her again, break the rules, will you? What good is it just watching over them? We need to protect them too."

He laid a hand on her shoulder. "She's stronger than you give her credit for."

Her face twisted into a grimace. "At least do something nasty to the boy."

Neale of the Ocean Winds stared at her levelly. "You know I'm not supposed to tell you anything, right?"

"Yes, I know. Loyalty is your virtue. So what is it you're not supposed to tell me but I have a feeling you will anyway?"

He pursed his lips together, and after a moment of consideration he gave a heavy sigh. "Secrets are for those with more energy. Nothing happened between Jet and the boy. He was spreading lies about having sex with her."

She clutched at his arm. "Jet needs to know."

"I think she always did. Things aren't always what they

seem. Sometimes a cry for attention is simply a cry for attention." He glanced over at the car that had just sped off. "I'll take good care of her. Nothing bad will happen, you have my word."

"I know this is a human thing to say, but thank you. If you hadn't shown up when you did Ben and I would have been stuck forever."

"Not my doing. Jet got away from me and I followed her, never guessing where we'd end up." He cast his gaze skyward. "Some things happen for a reason that even *we're* not meant to know."

Rachael followed his gaze skyward, becoming intrigued by the different shapes and colors of the clouds. Some resembled blobs of smeared paint. Others were like fat marshmallows. Some were thin wisps running across the sky that she suspected were broken angels, similar to the ones who'd trapped her in the art room.

"What are you looking at?" Neale asked her.

"Oh, I was just wondering why I knew nothing about a Purgatory for angels."

"You know as well as I do, we aren't privy to the way things are run."

"It still seems like something I should have known about." She gave him a piercing stare. "Did you know?"

He turned away. "I don't need to explain to you why I kept my mouth shut. Firstly I didn't know for sure it existed. Secondly, I'm a messenger just like you."

Rachael searched the clouds in the sky. "Does it have a name?"

Neale looked up. "I've heard rumors of a place called The Pale Echoes. I thought it was just talk."

Rachael wanted to be mad at the deception, yet now that she'd also been healed, she couldn't hold onto human emotions. "I screwed up with Ben. I was with him his whole life yet when it came right down to it, I didn't know him at all. I guess I should be lucky I'm getting this second chance."

Neale said nothing.

She took it as a sign that her statement was true. "Still, how many of us are unaware of the fate that awaits those who mess up? We have to do something to warn others."

He lowered his eyes and his voice. "It's not our place and you know it."

Like a trained actor he composed himself and blasted her with his dazzling smile.

"Right, I'd better be off before the little minx gets away from me again." He gave a merry laugh that shook the hair out of his eyes. Then his face became somber once more. "I hope to meet again under different circumstances."

Neale of the Ocean Winds vanished before she could tell him she'd like to meet him again, too.

She was alone once more and she hated it. So far, this period after Ben's ascension had been the longest downtime she'd ever had.

Mortals can keep their solitude, she told herself. Angels were created to be the constant watchdogs of humans, and she was desperate to get back to work. Work would stop her from dwelling on what other fate might have befallen her if, like an injured baby animal, she'd been left to fend for herself.

She gazed up at the sky once last time, unable to stop from wondering why Purgatory for angels was a secret. Milky white shapes like snow ghosts danced across the sky. Mesmerized, she found it difficult to steer her gaze away.

Ben used to agonize over the images he saw in the mirror. I can use the advice I gave Ben and simply *not look,* she told herself.

Thinking of Ben warmed her insides, but the warmth wavered and died. In time she would be able to remember him without heartache and guilt. She should not wish to suffer human emotions, but that she was to blame for his entrapment in the afterlife cloaked her in remorse.

Shaking her head, she cast aside her selfish concerns and turned her attention to the girl standing in the doorway. The girl was shaking, afraid to open the slip of paper that Jet had pressed into her hand.

When she whispered, the rustling sound of dead autumn leaves wafted down from the skies like feathers falling.

"Read it."

The young woman did as she was told and unfolded the note:

Dear Mom and Rachael

When a man gets scared he loses hope. And when he seeks it, he looks in the most unusual places. But he never looks within himself.

I wish I hadn't abandoned you both by running away to fight in a war I had no business fighting in. But wishing to change the past is like trying to carry a mountain on your shoulders. It wears you down. No man can change his past. He can only hope he is forgiven.

We all fall down. Sometimes we get back up and sometimes we don't. I ache knowing I'll never see you again. I ache to tell you I love you and to beg your forgiveness for leaving. Please know I'll be waiting for you on the other side. Make sure you come looking for me.

Your son and brother, Benjamin Andrew Taylor

"Read it to your mother," Rachael commanded gently. "The fog in her mind will be cleared long enough for her to grieve with you. She's waited years for her son to come home. The time has come for her to know the truth."

As though she had heard the angel, the woman nodded, turned, and went inside the house. While one part of the angel's mind was helping the old woman inside the house clear a path through her mental fog, another part lingered on the occupant of the car that had just left.

Jet would be okay, her angelic intuition sensed it. And she wasn't ruling out seeing Jet again one day. An angel could fly far and fast.

Not that angels were supposed to break the rule about using their divine powers to stalk mortals, or use them for any reason for that matter. She'd learned her lesson. No more messing with the plot, just focus on the job at hand and do it well. That would be its own reward.

Inside came the sound of the old woman sobbing. The pregnant girl moaned then she cried out in pain. The angel hurried inside and rolled up her sleeves. Her next assignment was entering the mortal world.

Many, many minutes later, as the angel gazed down at the cherub face she knew that *this* was her purpose. Not to watch the sky and wonder what Heaven might be like, but to watch over her mortal and make sure that he or she made it there.

ABOUT THE AUTHOR

D L Richardson is the author of character-driven science fiction for adults and paranormal fiction books for teens.

Whether DL is writing about ghosts, magic, the end of the world, alien invasion, curses, or guardian angels, all her books feature strong character development and lots of twists.

You won't find the usual tropes in her books. These are unique stories about regular characters who find themselves in difficult situations. And yes, lots of twists.

When she's not writing, she can be found, watching back-to-back episodes on Netflix, playing her piano or guitar, curled up on the couch reading a book, or walking the dog.

Stay up to date with new releases:
Sign up to the author newsletter for new releases, updates, special offers, and giveaways.

Details on the website
www.dlrichardson.com